THE MONDAY MUTINY

By the same author

Ninety Feet to the Sun
The Gemini Plot
Atlantic Encounter
The Eye of the Eagle
Secret of the Kara Sea

THE MONDAY MUTINY

A Ben Grant Story

Eric J. Collenette

WILLIAM KIMBER · LONDON

First published in 1987 by
WILLIAM KIMBER & CO. LIMITED
100 Jermyn Street, London SW1Y 6EE

© Eric J. Collenette, 1987

ISBN 0-7183-0665-1

This book is copyright. No part of it may be reproduced in any form without permission in writing from the publishers except by a reviewer who wishes to quote brief passages in a review written for inclusion in a newspaper, magazine, radio or television broadcast.

Photoset in North Wales by
Derek Doyle & Associates Mold, Clwyd
and printed in Great Britain by
Biddles Ltd, Guildford, Surrey

To my colleagues in
HMS TALYBONT   HMS CHIEFTAIN
HMS MERMAID
1947-1948

One

My tot is halfway to my lips when a thunderous knock on my office door jolts me out of my reverie and sloshes precious spirit over my knees. Before I can open my mouth to deliver a broadside the sliding door slams back on its stoppers and Leading Sickberth Attendant Albert Monday looms over me, breathing fire from his equine nostrils. I set the glass down on my desk and prepare to give him a blast, but he launches into me like a bloody tornado.

'He's got him doing bunny-hops on the fo'c'sle now – I thought you were going to have a word with him!' He is shaking with rage as he bears down on me. I have to lean well back to stay clear of his spittle.

'Who's got who doing what, for Christ's sake?' I demand. 'And what the hell do you mean by bursting in like this?'

'Petty Officer God Almighty Bold, that's who! He's got young Muir up there on the fo'c'sle with a rifle against the back of his knees doing bunny-hops. I warned you; that lad should be on light duties.' He is breathing hard as he thrusts his red face into mine.

Gritting my teeth I straighten up, forcing him back out into the passage. Ever since Monday came striding across the gangway to set up shop in *Condor*'s sick-bay he has been a pain in the arse. I've just about had a gut-full of his bloody nonsense. 'Watch your tongue,' I blare at him. 'You'll address me as "Coxswain" or "Chief", and you will wait to be asked in next time, or you'll find yourself at the captain's table – is that clear?'

He simmers down a bit, and that's the most you can hope for with this supercilious sod. There will be no backing down, for he treads a thin, uncompromising line with his disparaging attitude to the ways of the service.

'I made a report about Muir,' he says evenly, 'if anything happens to him you will have to bear the consequences – Swain.'

The way he spits out the word 'Swain' makes me cringe, but I bottle my temper with difficulty. 'We sent him ashore to see the quack, and he has a clean bill of health.'

'I don't believe it.'

I square up to him. 'Well you are just going to have to believe it, Monday. Now, get out of my sight before I lose my wool.'

He stares defiantly at me for a second or two, on the point of retaliating, then thinks better of it and slopes off muttering to himself. I snatch my tot and drain it without relish before deciding that I need some fresh air.

On deck I search out the one person I can talk to and find him outside the bos'n's store repairing a botched-up wire splice, while a nervous OD looks on wide-eyed. His thick, experienced hands are stripping the jute hearts out of the six strands ready to take the second tuck.

'Sometimes I wish I was back in submarines,' I complain bitterly.

He is reducing each strand by one third now. Like the OD I am fascinated by the deftness of his hands as he moulds the wire like an artist.

'The Navy knows best, Ben. When they say you are due for a spell in General Service they've got good reason.'

'I've had a run-in with Monday. I can't make up my mind about that bloke.'

'Neither can I. I reckon he's trouble, and if you don't do something about him you might regret it when we reach the Med.'

'That's easy to say,' I accuse.

He looks out across the anchorage. 'Ah yes, but I ain't

The Monday Mutiny

the coxswain, am I?' He changes tack. 'I never thought I would live ter see all those big bastards in one place at the same time,' he muses quietly, nodding out towards Portland Harbour at the battle-wagons swinging round their buoys.

HMS *Nelson, Anson, Howe, King George V*. They dominate the scene with their massive shapes, while dozens of scurrying liberty-boats ferry their animated cargoes to Weymouth for weekend leave.

Hordes of pink-faced kids in ill-fitting uniforms saunter about the place trying to look like veterans when they escape for a few hours from the rigid training in the ships. Unrelenting NCOs bully them in an endeavour to teach them the rudiments of seamanship so they can take the places of thousands of time-expired men waiting impatiently to get back into 'civvy street', now the war is over.

We received our lot a month ago. They came over the brow like nervous cattle and met me for the first time as I issued station-cards and gave a short lecture before sending them forward to join their new ship-mates. They were shown where to sling their hammocks and stow their gear, then they took part in a period of 'working up' to knock some of the rough edges away with drills and exercises that went on for weeks, and will continue for the time it takes us to reach Malta.

Hopefully, by then they will know their arses from their elbows, for we have a special job waiting for us when we get out into the Mediterranean. A task that many of us find hard to swallow. We will be tracking down Jewish illegal immigrant ships and trying to prevent them from reaching Palestine. I don't pretend to know the rights and wrongs of it, and having heard some of the yarns told by others who have returned from 'Haifa Patrol', it sounds a thoroughly unsavoury occupation. Women and kids are involved, and their elders become extremely hostile when their hopes are dashed by a group of matelots armed with long batons and automatics, who board their ships when they are within sight of the 'promised land' after months of tortuous journeying across land and sea.

My name is Ben Grant and I'm trying to come to terms with a new life in general service after a long spell in submarines. The ship is sailing for a two and half year commission and some of the married blokes are finding it hard to swallow, but, like me, the Navy frowns on marriage amongst the lower deck personnel, and although there has been some talk of 'married quarters', no one seriously believes that we will follow the army and air force with thousands of women and kids chasing their menfolk about: it would be too costly for a start.

I look at Robby again. He's married, but he reckons he has an arrangement with his missus – she doesn't complain about what she doesn't know, and neither does he. The Navy helps with occasional doses of bromide, but some find it hard to remain chaste, like Henry Ruscoe, the OA, who flits through the ship late at night with his arms full of bedding. Heading for the bathroom to shower and rinse out the results of over-active hormones.

Robby hands the splice back to the OD and we saunter aft together to stand in the lee of the Bofors gun deck, watching Petty Officer Bold lecturing the libertymen before they go down into the cutter. He is a jaunty, athletic type, with eyes that have a wild tinge when they look at you. I watch intently as he goes into his routine with arms braced to his sides and his back ramrod stiff. There is something about him that worries me. It is as though he needs a safety valve to release some of that pent-up energy boiling inside him.

'Yer leave expires at twenty-three fifty-nine, me buckos. Come back at midnight, and you're adrift. The first lieutenant ain't gonna listen ter yer bloody excuses. We've 'ad this year's quota of old ladies bein' rescued from burnin' buildings and the rest. We've even 'ad Stoker Trotter's tale abaht gettin' 'is foot caught in the tramlines and 'avin' ter walk ter the terminus ter get it aht.' He waits for the ripple of laughter to subside before continuing. 'The ship is under sailin' orders. Miss it, and yer'll be charged with desertion.'

'Quite a lad, ain't he?' snorts Robby.

I nod down at the gun-layer's badge on his arm. 'He's one of your lot, so you should know.'

His mouth tightens. 'All gunners ain't the same as him.' His weather-beaten face wrinkles up. 'We all know GIs can be full of wind and piss, but there is more to it with this bloke. I know something of his background. He was on one of the ships that took the Canadians into Dieppe – some of those lads came back with their minds bent.'

We lapse into silence with our thoughts running along the same lines. Some men would be better out of it now. Men like Bold who have had their minds destroyed. It doesn't show on the outside; especially when, like him, they are built like an advert for muscle magazines, and wear their caps at a rakish angle over a lean, lady-killing face. You have to live with someone like him for some time in the close confines of a small ship to notice the subtle, tell-tale signs. It worries me because I am the coxswain and should take my suspicions to the first lieutenant. Yet when it is all boiled down, what have I got to tell him? Bold carries out his duties to the letter. He doesn't drink, and turns out like a guardsman when there is need to put on a show. He might be a pain in the arse to his ship-mates, but as far as the wardroom is concerned he is a paragon of virtue.

The first lieutenant thinks Bold is bloody marvellous. Our 'Jimmy' is a strict disciplinarian who has fought his way up through the ranks, and seems to despise anyone who lacks his drive and ambition. He runs the ship like clockwork, and heaven help anyone who falls below par. It is a strange fact that many officers who come from the lower-deck are martinets with iron-bound ideas about how a ship should be run. Always looking for promotion, and becoming real bastards in the process. Jimmy is typical and tolerates only the best. His favourite saying when he sees a man fumble is, 'I've got a twelve-year-old daughter who could do better than that!' and everyone wonders what sort of muscle-bound amazon she must be. He has given up trying to persuade me to go for promotion and our relationship is somewhat strained.

Remote from all this our captain retains his dignity and distance by staying cloistered in his cabin when the ship is in harbour, only venturing abroad on occasional sorties to inspect Divisions, or carry out Captain's rounds on Saturday mornings, and of course to preside over his 'table' where he deals out punishment, promotion, and grants or refuses requests. He suits me for he handles the ship well, delegates authority, and is consistent, thorough and unbending when awarding punishment. The only flaw is his plummy voice and tofee-nosed attitude that rub many a raw nerve amongst the crew. One day he will be an admiral. Every contour of his haughty features spells that out; and he will get there without any undue effort.

The ship is a Bird Class sloop. Her main armament is three sets of twin four-inch multi-purpose quick firing guns – two forward, one aft. The quarterdeck is cluttered with depth-charge racks, and two sets of throwers on either side. Twin Bofors and oerlikons make up our secondary armament.

She is a plodder, designed to stay at sea for long periods on escort duty. Now and again she busts a gut to achieve eighteen to nineteen knots when we are in a hurry and the engine-room opens up the Parsons double-reduction geared turbines. Not very impressive when set beside the thirty-five knot destroyers, but those bastards are thirsty, needing to be suckled at frequent intervals, while *Condor* could take us to Malta with enough fuel left for a patrol.

I leave Robby and make my way forward. I could be going ashore with the rest but I know that I would be on that bloody train to Plymouth and end up outside her office like a lost puppy, waiting for her to leave, and this time I doubt if I would have the guts to refuse all she has to offer. It twists my guts to think she will find someone else, yet I know I would make a cock of things if I allowed my instincts to rule my brain and married her. Some of these bastards come to me with their paltry problems; talking as though I've got nothing between my legs, and cannot know what it is to want someone so much it tears your inside. Once we are at sea the pain will go away, and I will go back to dipping my wick from time to time like the rest, then I will deride my stupidity for ever getting serious over a woman.

I slide into my small office and sit staring into space for a moment. A sharp tap jerks me back to the present and I watch the door slide open. There stands Monday again with his serious eyes and dark complexion. He will look like a native when we get to Malta and he gets a tan.

'Can I speak to you for a moment, Swain?'

That's an improvement and I nod him inside. He eases his long six foot frame in while I back away from the desk to crane my neck to look up at him. He smells of the sick-bay, and his long-fingered hand clasps the ledge white-knuckled. He is an antiseptic sod who keeps himself to himself most of the time. A bit of a thinker this one, with a liking for classical music and heavy literature; making him an odd-ball in this crowd. He is efficient too, and skivers get short shrift when they try it on with him. He can lance a boil or search for crabs with the same detached expression, and he has no effeminate ways like many in his profession. I respect him for what he does, but like others I cannot get through to him. I know he has no real 'oppos' amongst the crew – after all, who wants to spend precious hours ashore visiting some lousy museum, or tramping off to visit a remote spot of historical interest, when all a matelot needs can be found on or near the waterfront?

He should be a petty officer by now, but he makes no secret of his contempt for what he considers to be archaic traditions implemented by morons like me. It is not surprising he has only a single anchor of a leading hand on his sleeve after laughing full in the face of a commander when he was being taken to task for overstaying shore-leave. It was the ritual that got to him. He just could not keep a straight face while the little pantomime of doffing his cap went on, and the Master-At-Arms bawled out the charge in a voice that shook the dockyard. Unable to control himself, he had exploded in front of everyone.

A note was entered on his service records and he was interviewed by his Divisional Officer in an attempt to find his motives. Monday denied any political convictions; stating that all he wanted was to run his department efficiently. No one was impressed, and I'm not really surprised. Even the way he wears his uniform is an affront, for he makes no effort to smarten it up, so it always looks as though it has just come out of its box; creased and ill-fitting. I spend much of my time telling him to get his hair cut and his shoes cleaned, but he continues to look scruffy.

'If it's about Muir, forget it,' I tell him coldly. 'We have all been chased round by GIs at one time or another. He can bring his complaints to me if he thinks he is being hard done by.'

He sniffs disdainfully. 'It isn't Muir, it's Stoker Petty Officer Seddon. I think he is going to desert.' His tone is expressionless. Completely matter-of-fact, as though making that bald report ends his responsibility.

I pull out the station cards and shuffle through them until I find Seddon's name. 'He is on forty-eight hours' leave – not due back until Sunday night. What makes you say that?'

'He as good as told me.'

'You'll need to explain more than that. Seddon is a professional man. Even if he was thinking of going on the trot, why should he tell you?'

He sighs heavily. 'He got spliced six months ago. He says there is no way he can stand separation for two and a half years.'

'Hard luck,' I sneer. 'He'll just have to grow out of it like

The Monday Mutiny

the rest of us.' I tap hard on the desk. 'It wouldn't do him any good anyhow. They will catch up with him the moment he goes home to his missus.'

For a moment he looks down at his feet, then back into my face, as though he has made a decision to tell it all.

'It is not that simple. I know he will regret it, but he says he has it all worked out with his wife. They will disappear together.'

I throw down the pencil in disgust. 'That's been tried many times. A man needs insurance cards and all kinds of other things to exist outside these days. He won't even be able to get a decent job.'

'Like you said, he isn't stupid. There's a small coaster tied up in Weymouth. She is an ex-Japanese landing-craft, called *Empire Seasilver*. Her skipper bought her as war surplus to make his fortune. Now he has realised his mistake and accepted some kind of deal with a foreign agent to run cargo off the West African coast – at least that's what he says. Personally, I think it's not as straightforward as that. Anyway, he needs an engineer and Seddon fits the bill. The idea is for them both to settle out there and make enough to set them up for life. Don't grin like that; to him it makes sense.'

My grin fades. I am taking it seriously now. 'He'll never be allowed to come home again.'

'He knows that. He says their life together is more important.'

A knot tightens inside as I get a vision of a bright-eyed face smiling up into mine, teasing me because I'm such a sobersides. Perhaps Seddon has a wife like that. 'It's bloody crazy!' I snarl. 'You still haven't told me why he told you all this.'

'He wanted me to go with them. He knows how I feel about the Navy.'

'And now you've split on him.'

'Have it your way – I just think he is heading for a lot of misery. The *Seasilver* is due to sail Sunday.'

The Monday Mutiny

'So what am I supposed to do about it?'

He shrugs. 'That's up to you. I thought you might try to persuade him not to be an idiot. You're more in his league than I am; maybe he will listen to what you have to say.'

'My bet is that he will see sense and come back as miserable as sin before we sail.'

'If you say so, Swain,' he says sardonically, and I feel anger welling up inside me.

'The Navy's just a bloody joke to you, isn't it? You don't really give a sod about Seddon; you just want to show how stupid we all are.'

His eyes go cold. 'I can't take a lot of it seriously, that's true. But as long as it feeds and clothes me, and, more important, takes me to places I could never afford to visit, it suits me fine. Especially when all I have to do in return is to run a sickbay for a crowd of blokes bursting with good health.'

I stand up, and he takes a step back as I confront him. 'In the meantime you'll spread your bolshie ideas through the ship. I'm not going to lecture you, Monday, but if I catch you trying to pass on your bloody nonsense to the new lads there will be trouble.' I ease off a bit. 'Now, get cleaned into your number ones and we'll go ashore on the eighteen hundred boat.'

'We!'

'That's what I said, and I warn you, this better not turn out to be a sod's opera.'

*

The waterfront at Weymouth is bleak and windy. Discarded newspapers skip across the open sand as waves wash in from the black shadows beyond the shoreline. A two-way stream of black-capped sailors hurry by to or from the liberty boats that use the end of the pier. We leave the main stream and walk along the harbourside, reading the names of small merchant craft moored alongside the wall. There is a channel packet laid up for the winter with her wartime paint scraped away and her gleaming red and black Great Western Railway funnel rising above clean white superstructure, while just astern of her a small coaster has the Blue Peter run up on her fore-mast to show she is about to sail for the Channel Islands.

After her comes a sad little vessel leaning disconsolately against the jetty, and I know before I read the faded legend on her bow that she is the one we are seeking. She is a blunt-nosed scow designed to run up on beaches, with a plain, square deckhouse aft and a small wheelhouse staring blankeyed across her cargo deck to a high fo'c'sle. She has no loading-ramp like our own landing-craft, and I can visualise Japanese marines spilling over her sides into the white sand of Philippine beaches. Her mooring wires hang slack and there is an air of neglect and dejection about her scruffy deck. She must be about seven hundred tons, with a single screw sticking half out of the water under her round stern.

There is no one about as I lead the way across a short gangway on to her cold, damp iron deck, and we make our way aft towards the wheel-house. Our footsteps must have wakened someone for a man leans out of a door to watch our approach. He is a small, black-jowled individual with close-cropped hair and a soggy cigarette hanging from his wet lips. He wipes his hands on a soiled towel, and there are bloodstains on the apron he is wearing below his pot belly. I cannot imagine what gastronomic delights this sea-cook produces for the crew, but he certainly destroys my appetite.

He studies us without speaking; his hostile eyes squinting from beneath thick brows that meet in the middle. Our uniforms are out of place on this rust-bucket, and she seems to breed filth everywhere we look. When I look past his boney shoulder into the galley any remaining dregs of appetite dissolve.

'We are looking for a man called Seddon,' I tell him, and he looks me up and down slowly before spitting his cigarette butt overside.

'Don't know anyone by that name.' The lie shows in his crafty eyes.

'Is your captain on board?'

'Nah.'

I glance over his shoulder again. 'You're cooking for someone. Is your engineer aboard then?'

His eyes flicker away for a second and he screws up the towel tightly, as though he would like to do the same to my neck. 'What's it to you? Who the hell are you, anyway?'

'I'm Seddon's ship-mate. I want a word with him, that's all.'

He throws the screwed-up towel on to the worktop. ' 'Ang on 'ere. I'll go below and see if anyone knows this Seddon bloke.' He jabs a finger down at my feet. 'You stay right 'ere, see?'

I nod and turn to look out across the fore-deck towards the creek that snakes away into the empty gloom of the open sea as he opens an inner door and we hear him clatter down a metal ladder.

'How'd you like to go to sea in this gash-barge, Monday?'

'You can't judge a book by its cover, Swain,' he grins. 'Alongside the living conditions of a corvette or a submarine she might be a little palace. It wouldn't surprise me if everyone has his own cabin.' I sniff. He knows bloody well what I mean, the obtuse bastard.

Late birds are swooping low across the metallic water, and several people are promenading their dogs along the opposite bank as the chill wind comes breathing in from the bay. The muffled roar of traffic carries from the town, and there is a noisy pub close by with yellow light spilling from its windows. I have never had much to do with Seddon; can't even recall his face properly, but now he has become all-important to me. Thanks to Albert Monday I have become involved in a man's private life, and I find myself standing on this flaking deck waiting to convince a man that he should leave his wife for two and a half years and probably risk his marriage. He has done his whack in the war, and now he thinks he has to run away in this disgusting little barge just so he can hang on to his wife.

The war has been over eighteen months, yet thousands still wait for demob while we train others as quickly as possible to take their places. That means experienced regulars like Seddon are more important than ever if we are to establish a good peace-time navy.

'Swain!' I turn to find him standing in the doorway looking at me, looking incongruous with his clean white shirt and smartly pressed trousers. 'You'd better come below.'

We follow him down into a flat where doors lead off into several cabins. In contrast to the sad state of her upper deck there is an atmosphere of cosy tidiness down here, and when Seddon opens his cabin door I see he has quarters on a par, if not better than most of *Condor*'s officers.

'Drink?' he offers, opening a small cabinet to display several bottles of spirit and an assortment of glasses. I shake my head and squat on the bench seat that runs across the after bulkhead.

'This isn't a social call,' I warn him.

He settles into a comfortable chair at one side of the folding table. It is fitted with fids and has a mahogany bookshelf running along the back filled with an assortment of paperbacks. A man could live cosy here, and to someone used to the snores and other intrusions from a messful of other men this seclusion must be luxury indeed.

'I didn't think it would be,' he says evenly, then looks up at me. 'I am still officially on leave, Swain. You have no right to come chasing after me like this, and as far as you're concerned I shall be back by Sunday night – whatever anyone might tell you.' He glares at Monday.

'Let us talk hypothetical then,' I suggest quietly. 'I'll have that drink now if you don't mind; it'll oil the hinges.' I watch his hands as he pours whisky into a tumbler. They look steady enough, but I can tell he is on edge and I take my time swirling the clean, clear liquid for a moment before taking a sip and savouring its sharp tang. 'Let's take a bloke like yourself who has worked his way up to petty officer and is on the verge of getting his chief's rate. It's downhill all the way for him now with the grinding years of climbing the ladder left well behind and a good crowd of mates to work with. A man like that would have to think deep before he threw it all down the gash-chute, I reckon.'

I look up to see him studying my face intently. The poor sod is torn apart; I can see it in his sad eyes. I look away again and drain the glass. The whisky sears my gullet with a satisfying sting, and he tops up my glass again without being asked while I go on. 'Let's face it, Seddon. There is no hiding place in the UK for a man on the run, so anyone with brains won't give it a thought; so what is the alternative?' I am looking hard into his face, ramming home every word. 'The British Merchant Service won't look at a deserter, so he needs to scratch about for some dodgy berth with a skipper who will try anything to get himself out of debt. A ship manned by chancers who can't get legitimate jobs. There isn't much future in that; just years of exile, hoping that one day there will be an amnesty for deserters. Some bloody existence that would be!'

The outside noises seep in through the open port as he pores over my words. 'This hypothetical bloke, Swain. What if he thinks he has done more than his stint already? Perhaps he's still got six years of his twelve to do and feels that the signature of a sixteen-year-old kid shouldn't be enough to take away a man's liberty for that long. Perhaps he thinks two and a half years is too long to take someone away from his family in peacetime. Kids of eighteen saying goodbye to their families, to come back aged twenty after swannin' round some of the gut-rotting swill holes of foreign ports. A year, or even eighteen months, is more than enough I reckon. There's always the hard-nosed volunteers for the longer spells; blokes who don't give a sod for home anyway.'

The Monday Mutiny

I stand up and set the glass hard down on the table. 'Thanks for the lecture and the booze, Seddon. I'll say only this. If this bloke we are talking about has any sense he will be back on board before his leave expires Sunday night. After our little talk I feel obliged to mention my concern to the first lieutenant, unless I get some kind of reassurance in good time. If I have to make that report I can see this little barge being stopped before she reaches the three-mile limit.'

'You can't stop a merchant packet just like that.'

'Don't bet on it, Seddon. If the Navy has reason to believe she is doing something illegal she will be stopped.' I lean into him as I stress, 'That's one of the peacetime functions of the service; or didn't you know?'

'She isn't doing anything illegal.'

'With a deserter on board she is. Think about it.' I turn to leave and run smack into a tall, fair-haired man wearing a high-necked blue sweater under a black reefer.

'Who the hell do you think you are, shouting and laying down the law on my ship?' His voice is educated but hard as he glares at me with angry eyes. He is a seaman all right; it shows in his weather-worn features and brawny hands. There is nothing shifty about him either; not the type you expect to find involved in shady dealings with a bunch of crooks. He shifts his stare to Seddon. 'What's the trouble, chief?'

'No real problem, Skipper. Just some mates of mine who have got hold of the wrong end of the stick.'

'Didn't sound like that to me. You know damn well I don't like a lot of strangers coming on board.'

'I didn't know they were coming until they turned up. No time to let you know.'

For a moment he looks us over as he weighs up the situation. 'Right then. Get about your own affairs, and next time you want to visit have the courtesy to let me know in advance. It is not polite to walk on to a ship without being asked.'

He must have heard the tail end of our conversation, yet he is standing aside full of confidence, allowing us to slide past. The cook grins at me as I climb out on to the upper deck. One final look shows everything battened down ready for sea, and something makes me look hard at the hatch-covers. Somehow they don't fit in with the slovenly state of the rest of her; they are too taut and secure. I would expect old canvas with wrinkles and ragged holes, yet these are smooth and unblemished. There isn't even a seam that I can see, and I run my hand casually across the flat surface as we make our way towards the gangway. It is not canvas at all. It is a steel cover, welded down to the rim of the coaming, and it makes no sense. Even in the gloom I can see there is no way to open up and work ordinary cargo. Whatever this ship carries must get in and out of her holds some other way.

I search about quickly and find the shadowy shapes of two tall ventilators outlined against the purple sky. I am about to move closer to investigate further when I realise I am being watched from the bridge, and when I look back I see Seddon and the skipper staring down at me. That makes me change my mind and go ashore quietly to follow Monday along the road. Ventilators don't necessarily mean a live cargo. Other goods need air too, but put that together with the sealed hatch-covers and it adds up to living accommodation.

'Palestine!' I breathe aloud.

'What?' Monday's voice cuts into my thoughts.

'That bloody ship isn't going anywhere near the west coast of Africa. She's a bloody illegal immigrant: I'd bet my pension on it. I reckon they have gone as far as they dare to convert her without arousing suspicions ashore, but you can bet she will have extra latrines and lifeboats rigged as soon as she gets to a friendly port. Christ! I'd give my right arm to see what's under those sealed hatches. My guess is the holds are fitted out with bunks for the poor sods who will be conned into sailing with her. What a bloody nightmare that journey will be!'

'How can you be so certain? There must be plenty of other

The Monday Mutiny

reasons for the way she is rigged. Perhaps she has tanks fitted – they would require ventilation, wouldn't they?'

I ignore him. 'That bastard Seddon! He knows damn well we are bound for Haifa. That puts him on the other side. He's a lousy traitor!'

Monday stops in his tracks; staring at me with a derisive expression. 'Traitor! That's a bit strong isn't it? You're not even sure that ship is going to the Med.'

'Oh that's where she's going all right. What else do you call a man who deserts his ship and joins the other side? Christ, he knows all sorts of things that could be useful to the Hagana!'

'Hagana?'

'That's the mob who arranges these trips to the "promised land". They are busy shooting our squaddies in Palestine right now, and trying to chase Arabs out of their own country. That stupid, self-centred sod has joined them.' I set off at a fast pace, leaving him to trail astern.

'Where are you going?' he asks breathlessly.

'Back to the ship as quickly as possible – I've got to see Jimmy right away.'

He stops in his tracks again, and when I look back he is watching me reproachfully.

'Are you coming?' I yell at him.

'You are going to report Seddon?'

'I'm going to do no more than make a report,' I state firmly. 'Then it's up to Jimmy. There is more to this now than just trying to stop a bloke making an idiot of himself. If I say nothing I'm as guilty as he is.'

'Well you can fucking well do it on your own,' he explodes.

I don't even bother to reply. I'm so incensed I spend hard-earned cash on a taxi all the way round Chesil Beach to Portland and bribe the coxswain of another ship's cutter to drop me off at our gangway.

The first lieutenant's in his cabin when I hammer at his door. 'Come in,' he responds, and I can almost hear him wince at my uncouth barrage, but I'm in no mood for gentle, polite raps.

I find him seated at his small desk with some paperwork spread out and an annoyed expression on his face. He listens as I explain and doesn't blink an eyebrow when I tell him about the sealed hatch-covers and the vents. When I'm done he leaves me standing in a vacuum for some time feeling stupid while he ponders over what I've told him.

'Who knows about this apart from yourself and Monday?' he asks in a guarded tone.

'No one, sir.'

'Sit down, Grant.' He indicates a chair and I squat with my cap twisting agitatedly in my hands. 'You should have come to me before going off like that. What did you hope to achieve?'

'I thought I might talk him out of deserting, sir.'

'I see. Well I'm afraid you jumped the gun. However, you can leave it with me.' He looks down at his papers for a moment, then asks quickly, 'Is Monday on board?'

'Yes, sir.'

'Tell him I wish to see him immediately. In the meantime say nothing of this to anyone. I'm certain you have read too much into the situation, Grant. Perhaps next time you will remember to come and ask before you go off half-cocked.'

'But, sir!' I gasp.

'That's all, Coxswain.' My mouth opens and closes soundlessly. 'I said, that's all,' he repeats, nodding towards the door.

On the upper deck the wind whines through the rigging and scuffs up the surface of the harbour, driving white horses down our side as *Condor* snubs at her bridle. I slide down the ladder on to the quarterdeck where the quartermaster and his bos'n's mate huddle in their corner. The light above their heads casts long shadows across the glossy paintwork and glints on the big, brass nameplate. Robby is out on deck for a final breath of air before turning in.

'What do you want me ter do wiv yer gear when you're gorn?' he chaffs.

'Eh?'

'You look like you're goin' ter take your final dive.'

'Some of the things that go on in this man's navy is enough to make anyone take a dive,' I grate through clenched teeth. 'No bastard gives a sod for anything these days.'

'You only just found that out?' he chortles. 'Want ter tell old Robby abaht it?'

'It'd make you choke,' I snarl, and stalk off.

Two

The skipper starts his rounds at eleven o'clock, and puts everyone's back up. Firstly because it means that tot time will be delayed for an hour, and secondly because most departments have their key ratings away on weekend leave. This will be the last inspection before we sail so he is finicky, peering into every obscure corner, running a wet finger along ledges, and examining food lockers as though they harbour every parasite in the book. It is no use trying to blind him with bullshit either. Utensils arranged in 'tiddly' patterns on scrubbed tables, or polishing the cutlery until it sparkles will not deter him, nor cover up what lies beneath the façade. He orders hammocks to be pulled out of their stowage-racks to reveal unscrubbed ones that have been strategically buried out of sight in the centre by feckless owners who will find themselves on report.

In a ship where men must live cheek by jowl in the hot climate of the Mediterranean hygiene is paramount, and he intends to have things right from the outset. I lead the procession through the ship in time-honoured fashion; piping the 'still' as we enter each compartment. Those in charge make their reports, then take note of his complaints. In one mess a total rescrub is ordered just because their small 'pussers' cases are not stowed uniformly, and that is quite serious for a man who hopes to catch an early train for a short weekend with his family.

When we emerge on to the upper deck there is no let-up at all. Robby wilts under the full weight of his captain's cynicism, as does Petty Officer Bold when the guns undergo a thorough inspection. A slack lashing on the port whaler, a rope's end not cheesed down correctly, a dirt scupper, a loose tompion; there is nothing that misses the master's keen eye. One after another the faults are ticked off until we arrive on the signal-deck.

As we go by the twenty-one inch lamp there is a loud belch from inside the locker beneath its mounting. I'm nearest, so I jerk open the steel door to reveal Signalman Cummings, the ship's drunk, twisted into a ball inside his hideaway. He blinks out at us like a startled owl, trying to focus into the blinding daylight. No one utters a sound as he painfully eases his body out of the cramped quarters to stand in his creased, filthy uniform and crumpled cap, desperately striving to regain his composure.

This bloke is a disaster. He cannot be trusted ashore on his own, and I had him on my list for being adrift. How he was overlooked when his mates cleaned up for 'rounds' beats me. Possibly because this is his own sector and everyone was too busy to check, or cover up for him. Now he totters with his eyes screwed up, unshaven, dishevelled, and putty-faced with hang-over. I can smell the stale booze from eight feet away, and his hands shake uncontrollably as he makes a vain effort to stay at attention under the collective glare of the assembly. Even our captain is lost for words adequate for the occasion, so he just eyes the signalman up and down before moving off, leaving me to grate through clenched teeth, 'Report to my office with your cap in your hand, Cummings.'

After that everything else is an anti-climax and the ship returns to Saturday routine with the hands piped to a 'make and mend' after dinner. Senior hands compare notes with the first lieutenant on the quarterdeck, then go off to slate negligent leading hands, leaving Jimmy and me to tidy up the loose ends. As he runs a finger down his list I glance up to look out over the breakwater towards the bay.

'That's the *Empire Seasilver*, sir.'

He follows my outstretched arm to study the insignificant little vessel as she creeps out towards the open sea. She looks even more decrepit as she thrusts blunt bows into a choppy sea.

'You don't know for certain that Seddon is on board, Grant.'

'If you say so, sir,' I respond sourly.

He gives me a sharp look. 'I won't tolerate insolence, Coxswain.'

'Didn't mean to be, sir. It's just that I am sure he is in that ship, and I reckon she is on her way to Palestine. Once she gets outside the three-mile limit we can't touch her. It don't seem right somehow.'

'I have already told you that I will take care of it,' he snaps angrily. 'You have done your duty by reporting it to me; now forget it, and get on with the more immediate task of bringing that damned signalman to his senses. Who is Officer of the Watch?'

'Lieutenant Border, sir.'

'Good; he'll know how to deal with it. I want that man on Captain's Report as quickly as possible.' He looks at me. 'I don't understand how he managed to get back on board without anyone knowing, Coxswain.'

I make no comment. Most probably he was too drunk to come over the ladder in the full glare of the duty watch, so he may have persuaded the bowman of the cutter to hide him under the forward canopy until they tied up at the boom, hoping to sober up enough to collect his station card before morning. I shudder to think of the drunken antics that must have taken place as he scrambled over the bouncing prow of the small boat and climbed up the Jacob's ladder to get inboard without being observed. I will have a few choice words with the cutter's coxswain when I see him.

'That's all, Coxswain.' Jimmy's order shakes me back to the present, and I am about to leave when he adds, 'I want a good turn-out for Sunday Divisions tomorrow. We must try to make up for this bloody fiasco. No one is excused. I expect the captain will wish to say a few words after the church service.'

'Aye aye, sir.' I salute and turn away. That scruffy little ship is bucketing out past the 'Bill'. No doubt Seddon is nursing her engine to put as many miles as possible between us and them before his leave officially expires. I see no earthly reason why we cannot stop her, and Jimmy's attitude makes no sense at all.

When I go below I expect to find Cummings waiting for me so that I can take him before the Officer of the Watch to have him charged. He is nowhere in sight and I storm into the communications branch mess breathing fire.

'Sparks' Wilson shoves his monstrous beard at me. 'What time's bubbly comin' up, Swain?'

'Where's Cummings?' I pretend I haven't forgotten the bloody rum; there will be a bloody riot if I don't issue it soon.

'In the sickbay.' Wilson is chewing at something, with his beard jumping up and down. It is an unruly growth that should never be allowed, growing in total confusion with compact ringlets like uncoiled springs spiralling in profusion as they bounce with every movement of his jaw. Everyone from the skipper down has had a go at him about it, and to give him his due he makes an effort to control it, but no amount of trimming will keep it in check and it explodes in all directions. Any suggestion that he should shave it off sends him into a black depression, so we have learned to live with it.

'What is he doing in the sickbay?' I ask suspiciously.

' 'E reckons 'e might 'ave caught the boat up.'

'Cummings is never in a fit state to catch a dose,' I snort. 'Off you go and tell Monday I want Cummings in my office in thirty minutes or they will both be in the rattle.'

That gives me time to deal with the rum, and I find Lieutenant Border fuming impatiently when I get to the rum-store. I try to ignore him as the dark liquid is measured out into the fannies. The tangy aroma sets my taste-buds going and I decide to go down for my tot before attending to the signalman. Some of my bad humour fades as I contemplate a quiet afternoon with my head down after I've crashed out the set of underwear I have on and showered away the sweat. When I reach my office Cummings is not there.

'Jesus Christ!' I explode, slamming the door shut and hustling forward to the sickbay. Inside I find the signalman reclining luxuriously in a chair with a small glass of white liquid in his hand while he gazes up at me with an inane grin splitting his stupid face.

Monday comes out from his inner sanctum. 'Sorry, Swain,' he apologises. 'I was just coming to report. Didn't reckon you would finish the rum issue so quickly.'

'Report what?' I ask dangerously. 'I ordered him to come to my office immediately. You should know by now that that means yesterday. So why is he still sitting here on his fat arse?'

'He's ill.'

I look at the degenerate signalman sitting there with his blank expression, exuding whisky fumes into the antiseptic atmosphere. It is hard for me to accept that this is one of our best bunting tossers, capable of rattling away on a lamp at a speed that sends many a less able recipient into despair. On the bridge he is master of his profession: ashore, or in the mess he becomes a liability.

'Ill?' I demand aggressively. 'What's wrong with him that twenty-one days' detention won't cure?'

'Bad news I'm afraid, Swain. I am going to have to send him to Bighi. In my opinion he is unfit to go to sea.'

I give Monday a withering look. 'I repeat; what is wrong with him?'

'Delirium tremens – DTs. You can see the way he is shaking, and he is hallucinating.'

'DTs!' I exclaim with an ironic laugh. 'DTs! Monday, this bloke has bin arsing about in a semi-daze for fucking years. He's a joke on the messdeck. Two weeks ago I had to tear down a notice from above the cubicle in the heads – do you know what it read?'

He shakes his head and I sweep my arm across as though I'm pointing out the wording. ' "These stalls are reserved for Godfrey's Gnus" it said. Godfrey is his Christian name. Believe me, he will be as right as rain as soon as he has had his tot.'

I direct my attention to the signalman. 'Get along to my office at once, Cummings. You will be on stoppage of leave, pay and spirits long enough to dry out if there is any justice.'

'I'm sorry, Swain, but I must insist that he stays here until he has seen a doctor. He has reported sick and I am not satisfied he is malingering. I will not accept responsibility for allowing him to go without an expert examination.'

'You will do as you are told, lad.'

'In that case I request to see the captain.'

'That's your right, laddy, but right now this bloody skate is going to duff his lid to the Officer of the Day. Get moving, Cummings, and no more of your nonsense – *move*!'

He staggers to his feet with an old-fashioned leer at the SBA, then leads out into the messdeck with me chivvying him up from behind. He sways with a far-away expression on his face while I read out the charge to Border. This is all old-hat to the signalman, and he doesn't bat an eyelid when he is put on First Lieutenant's Report.

I march him back to my office and take away his station card. He will receive something like seven days' number elevens – stoppage of leave and pay, besides having to turn to during off-duty hours for extra work. By the time he has served his sentence we should be in Malta, so he will probably miss only one run ashore in Gibraltar, and the worst part of it as far as he is concerned is to miss his rum, but if I know his mess-mates there will be a whip-round at tot time to make up for that. You can't win with scoundrels like Cummings.

I follow him back to his mess and stand discreetly in one corner while he joins his mates. His last tot sits waiting for him. Half a cup of grog – two-thirds water and one of rum – which he takes in both hands, to gloat over it for a moment before he lifts it with shaking hands to drink it dry in one, long, satisfying gulp.

Back in my office I sit and study his station card for a moment before stowing it inside a drawer. He will shape up once we get into sea-routine I tell myself. He has been like this before and will be again. There are plenty of his sort, and we have to live with their bloody nonsense. Later, when I get the chance, I'll report Monday's concern to the first lieutenant, just to get the LSBA off the hook if the signalman does anything stupid, but that is as far as I will go.

As regards the request to see the skipper: any matelot has the right to go to the highest authority if he persists, but the mechanics are slow and cumbersome, designed to put off all but the most dedicated dissenter. Somehow I don't think Monday will get further than his divisional officer.

Apart from a few rebels like Cummings the ship's company is a good one, and Sunday morning sees them turned out in their number ones for divisions. If Jimmy had his way this is the moment for the skipper to give his pre-sailing pep-talk, but he doesn't bother; probably because a third of the men are still ashore, and we have taken on board an intelligence officer who will speak to us when we are at sea, to try to explain why we are being sent to Palestine.

All that is in the future, however, and for the time being we get down to the final preparations for slipping our buoy on the morrow. I post the daily orders announcing that 'Special Sea Dutymen' will close up at ten thirty so that we can go to 'Stations for leaving harbour' at ten forty-five.

The wind is kind to us and eases to a gentle breeze with the sun drying the deck with its wintry glow. By mid-morning the bridle is unshackled and we are riding to

The Monday Mutiny

the slip-rope. The ship's postman is on board and the cutter hooked on to the falls ready for hoisting. I can make my routine report to the first lieutenant, 'Ship's company on board, sir; except for ERA Seddon – He is still adrift, I'm afraid.' I keep my face expressionless.

'Very good, Coxswain,' he responds wooden-faced, and goes off to make his own report to the captain. I shrug and go to find the two telegraphsmen waiting for me in the wheelhouse, while all the sounds of a ship making last minute preparations for sea drift in from outside our little metal box. There is an open scuttle in front of me when I am at the wheel, through which I can see over 'B' gun to part of the fo'c'sle.

The crew is well drilled and could carry out this routine blindfolded, providing the 'new entries' are kept well out of their way. They will adapt in time to become useful, but right now they are better employed where they will do least harm, so we use them to hoist the boats and man the side while we make our exit under the critical gaze of the big ships. Everything has to be done the 'pusser' way today, so we stretch out the boat falls along the deck and hoist by hand, the way Nelson would have appreciated. At other times we do it the more practical way by running the falls through snatchblocks to the winch.

It's all being done for effect today with three bos'n's mates standing on the director platform, ready to pipe the 'still' as we go by the other ships in the anchorage. Right up in the eye of the ship a seaman is waiting to whip down the Union Jack the moment the slip is knocked off to release us from the buoy. Everyone is on show today as we wait for the captain to arrive on the bridge, take stock of wind and tide, then with a short gesture of his hand signal the fo'c'sle to let go. The maul crashes down and the slip-rope snakes out through the fairlead. The ship is free and the buoy surges back on its moorings as the wind takes us to starboard with no need of the screws to swing her clear.

'Slow ahead together!' The first vibrations from the

engines transmit through the soles of my shoes and I feel her respond to the rudder.

'Starboard ten – Midships – Meet her – Steer one five one.' A glance up from the compass repeater shows the gate in the breakwater dead ahead as the pipes trill the first salute, to be answered by the brassy sound of a bugle. That will be HMS *Nelson* with her company facing to starboard at attention, watching us slide past, many of the trainees standing on a ship's deck for the first time in their lives, wondering what it must be like to sail away to a world they have never seen.

The lectures start during the afternoon. A series of half-hour talks delivered by a stern-faced officer to each watch as they come off duty. As far as I am concerned, I'm just as confused by the whole affair as I was before he began, for it is much too big a subject to cover in such a short time.

It has something to do with promises made by the British way back in the first world war, and what the Jews reckon to be their God-given right to a chunk of the Middle East.

'There is plenty of room either side of Jordan for both races to live together,' he says soberly. 'I do not need to remind you of how much the Jewish people have suffered during the past few years. Many of the immigrants are "displaced persons", with nowhere to call home. However it would be wrong to allow thousands, even millions, of them to pour into a country which, though primitive, has been occupied by Arabs for centuries: Palestinians value their way of life as much as we do. A compromise is being worked out. Our job is to police the situation and restrict the inflow of illegal immigrants. You may be asked to carry out some very unpleasant duties.

'There will be desperate people determined to do everything they can to make things difficult for you; and to prepare you for this, a special fortnight's training has been arranged in Ghain Tuffieha at Malta where you will be taught how to jump safely from one ship to another, then get to your allotted stations so that the ship can be taken into custody. The Jews will use steam hoses, steel knitting needles; in fact any weapon they can lay their hands on to repel you. You will be under extreme pressure in hazardous conditions, but you must not over-react, nor retaliate in an undisciplined manner. That is what the training is all about.'

He goes on for a while before asking for questions, and it is quite plain to me that the audience is no wiser than I am at the end of it all. I suppose we tell ourselves that if the Navy says it must be done, then it must be okay. Only Leading Sickberth Attendant Monday seems to have serious doubts.

'Don't try to figure it out,' I advise him. 'The golden rule is just to get on with your job and forget politics; you know that.'

'You know, Coxswain,' he says with a sardonic twist to his mouth, 'I bet every Nazi war criminal says the same thing – "I only did as I was told" – as though that excuses everything.'

I bristle. 'What makes you think you know it all, Monday? Don't you think it is just possible we are stopping a bloodbath by preventing a sudden flood of Jews into Palestine? Could be we are taking the heat out of a dangerous situation.'

'We shouldn't be poking our bloody noses in at all; it's nothing to do with us.'

I turn away from him and snarl something about getting on with his job. A breath of fresh air is what I need, and I go up top to find PO Bold putting 'A' gun's crew through their paces.

The loading-numbers are clutching dummy rounds close to their chests while he stands back to bellow at them.

'Sixteen rounds a minute is normal, but we are going ter work up to eighteen or you will sweat blood, believe me!' His voice rises to a shriek. 'Stand to aircraft starboard! Angle of sight four five!' The muzzles lift together as they swing right towards their imaginary target. This has the effect of lowering the breeches until the loading numbers have to crouch down with their elbows almost touching the deck to punch the shells into the breeches. This is 'fixed' ammunition with shell and cartridge combined into single units making them heavy and clumsy to handle from this position, but despite this they are getting into their stride quickly, and although each round has to be extracted instead of being automatically ejected they seem to me to be keeping up a very good rate of fire.

It doesn't satisfy Bold however. He studies his stop watch with a sour expression and counts the rounds like a doctor checks a pulse.

'Fourteen!' he thunders at the sweating men. 'Bloody useless – like a lot of languid lesbians, you lot!' A large vein pumps in his neck and his face grows purple as he rails on. Gunnery NCOs are not noted for their sophisticated repartee but this bloke is beyond anything I've seen before. The captain of the gun is a newly rated PO still dressed in bell-bottoms and a square collar while he goes through his probationary period and feeling his way carefully. He is unwilling to make a stand against the belligerent gunner in case he should make a fool of himself, even though he and Bold share the same mess. When the drill is over he should take the other man aside and have a word with him, but I know he won't when I observe the desperation in his face.

I shrug and move off; it is not for me to interfere. After all, there is nothing wrong with trying to get the best out of a gun's crew, and we have all suffered barbaric tongue-lashings from GIs and gunners' mates at one time or another. Somehow, though, they always seemed to keep control of themselves no matter how vicious their language, whereas Petty Officer Bold shakes and splutters as though he is the verge of a breakdown. I leave him to it.

The days are short now, and the wind brings the breath of winter in from the Atlantic as we sail southward towards the Bay of Biscay. A blood-red sunset illuminates the sky ahead, turning the superstructure black in silhouette as she bucks the short seas. Astern the ocean folds away into a dark mystery while across the bows I gaze across a vast golden prairie stretching to infinity. The ship rolls easily, and her vitality pulses beneath my feet as I relish the feel of her. I stand alone on the Bofors gun deck, tasting the acrid tang of exhaust from the funnel as it cuts into the clean wind she is making for herself. It is a moment to hold on to, when nothing matters but your own thoughts and the sensual movement of the ship, while most of her company are below decks, and I am left with the sounds and sensations of the sea as she spreads her wake aft into the growing darkness. It clears the mind and elevates the soul. I have seen it a thousand times before but on the first evening at sea it has a special quality.

' 'Ave yer seen the coxswain?' The voice comes from just below on the maindeck.

'Nah, and I don't fuckin' want to.'

'Well if yer do, tell 'im Jimmy wants ter see 'im in 'is cabin. Can't think where the old bastard's got ter. Praps someone's slung 'im over the side; that's the best place fer coxswains, I reckon.'

I grin to myself. I can place the voice now. It belongs to one of the new bos'n's mates, fresh out of training and full of himself. Trying to emulate his more experienced shipmates. I wait for them to move off before I climb down the steel ladder. The majesty is gone from the sky now and I duck through the bulkhead door into the stuffy smells of the ship as I go down to the first lieutenant's cabin.

'Come!' he invites in response to my knock, and he is looking up at me when I slide open the door. I straddle my legs each side of the coaming while he takes his time.

'ERA Seddon's kit is to be stowed in the sloproom. Will you see to it at once please, Coxswain?'

'Aye aye, sir.' I stand waiting for more and he swivels his chair so that he faces away, then snaps an impatient look over his shoulder.

'Well that's all, Grant. Get on with it.'

All be buggered! I am thinking to myself. A man is absent without leave – a deserter now that he has missed his ship. I stand my ground and insist, 'Sir. That is not all, begging your pardon. This will have to be reported to the shore authorities so that they can make enquiries and have him arrested when the ship calls at a friendly port. He is on the run now, sir. Only last week two blokes were brought back from France when they tried to jump ship. I'd say it is most urgent that we make that report immediately, sir.'

For a moment I think I've stuck my neck out too far and prepare for a tongue-lashing when he shapes up to me, but then he seems to relent, looking away for a moment and leaning back in his chair. He indicates the leather-covered seat fixed to the bulkhead. 'Shut the door and sit down.' His voice has a softer edge to it; almost a conspiratorial quality as he searches for the right words. I slide in quietly and sit with my cap twisting in my lap.

'Seddon is not a deserter, Coxswain. In fact quite the reverse. I don't want reports going anywhere.' He looks straight at me. 'The captain and I had hoped to keep this confidential; only a few people know what is going on and we would have liked to keep it that way. Now I see you are too long in the tooth to be fobbed off, so I want your solemn promise that what I am about to tell you will go no further.'

He waits for my nod before going on. 'As far as the ship's company is concerned Seddon is on the run and all the usual steps are being taken to get him back. We have tried to make it as plausible as possible, but we did not count upon your finding out about the *Empire Seasilver*. To set the scene, Seddon had to appear to take someone into his confidence and he chose Monday because he thought he would be the one who would keep his mouth shut until the ship sailed. Seddon told him about the *Seasilver* and the new life he and his wife hoped to live together, and it seemed the SBA was convinced.'

He throws a pencil down unto the desk, watching it roll

across to the side. 'Well, he must have had second thoughts, and you know the rest.'

'Yes, sir. I'm still puzzled though.'

'Patience!' he barks angrily. 'If it had not been for your damned impetuosity I would not have to explain at all.' He simmers down again. 'We know the Hagana have two 5,000-ton ships converted to carry the biggest crowd of illegal immigrants yet to sail for Palestine. The *Empire Seasilver* is to be used only as a tender, picking up parties from various secret places and ferrying them out to the larger ships which will stay outside territorial waters. The whole set-up is made even more delicate because both these freighters are American owned, and the USA takes a very different view of the situation than we do. If we break international rules we could land ourselves in a lot of trouble. Therefore it is essential for us to know where these ships are at all times, for once they are loaded they will be shadowed all the way to Palestine, and once inside the three-mile limit every available ship will be used to apprehend them. We are convinced that this is their big effort, and that if we stop these ships from delivering their cargoes we will have dealt a vital blow and probably persuaded them to have patience and do it our way. Seddon is an important part of the whole plan, Grant.'

'What happens if they rumble him, sir?'

He looks uncomfortable. 'There is no reason why they should if we play our part. Anyway Seddon has no illusions – he knows the risks involved – he is a very brave man.'

'So all that bumph about being newly wed was just part of the hoax?'

He looks away again. 'No; that is true enough. It is part of the deal in fact.' He shuffles papers about on his desk. 'You see by doing this he will effectively miss the commission, and we have promised him that he will spend the next two years or so in the Home Fleet.'

I stand and clamp my hand on the door-handle. 'May I go now, sir?'

The Monday Mutiny

He nods, still without looking at me, but I know he can feel my eyes boring into him as I sidle out into the passage. This then is the peace-time Navy, and the new world where everyone will live in harmony. Women and kids stowed away in stinking-holds, bribery, treachery, cheating. Whatever happened to the regattas, showing the flag in friendly foreign ports with parties on the quarterdeck and coloured lights rigged on the awnings on balmy summer evenings? Somehow I think that era belongs to the thirties, never to be seen again.

When I go on deck the night is black and the wind is growing to build hefty waves that slash the ship's side. I recognise the signs. Tomorrow we will be in the Bay, and despite the beautiful sunset it is going to live up to its evil reputation.

Three

Malta seems much as I left it in 1942, except that someone has cleared away most of the rubble and filled some of the gaps with new houses. Brown-skinned masons are everywhere, shaping big square stones to rebuild the bombed buildings, and if you look carefully at their tired, lean features you can read the aftermath of the long siege.

In Dockyard Creek a destroyer lies rusting and abandoned with her bows missing, looking as though she has been sliced like a loaf of bread just forward of her bridge with entrails of pipes and ventilation shafts growing out of the sealed-up bulkhead. This is no wartime relic. This is HMS *Saumarez* who survived the war to become part of the peace-time Navy until she sailed through the narrow channel between Corfu and Albania where she hit a mine. Her consort HMS *Volage* went to help and blew her own bows off on another mine. Who was responsible is still in question, but few doubt that it was the Albanians, for they are not keen on our ships using the narrow channel that brings them so close to their shoreline.

Forty-odd blokes died that day, many of them veterans who were waiting for their demob numbers to come up. Now a solemn ceremony takes place each anniversary at their graveside. *Volage* is at sea again, but HMS *Saumarez* is considered not worth the cost of repairs.

Grand Harbour is full of ships, and on the other side of Valletta other creeks shelter smaller units of the Mediterranean Fleet. Of special interest to me is HMS *Wolfe*, the submarine depot ship which dominates Msida

The Monday Mutiny

Creek as she nurses her brood of T and S boats. All looking very smart in their Mediterranean blue paintwork. HMS *Wolfe* is the ex-Canadian Pacific liner *Montcalm* with her name diplomatically altered to suit her new owners.

I meet some of my old shipmates ashore who tell me they have a good life now. Their only grouse is that they do not travel about as much as the rest of the Fleet because they are used as clockwork mice for the frigates and destroyers; day-running from Malta; returning each evening to the depot-ship. Until recently there was compensation in lying opposite the building on the side of the creek which housed WRENs. Unfortunately someone spotted the raised periscopes trained in their direction and spoiled the whole thing.

In yet another creek HMS *Woolwich* is berthed alongside Manoel Island. She looks after some of the destroyers, sloops and frigates, while trots of landing craft, trawlers, and an assortment of obsolete war-weary vessels crowd the backwaters, waiting to sail home to the breakers with companies of eager men, waiting to get out into civvy-street now that the Navy has no use for them. It is a changing service, dragging itself back to its peacetime glory, and this motley array of nondescript craft have no part in it.

We find plenty of room in Sliema Creek to secure to head and stern buoys, for it is a busy time as increasing numbers of immigrant ships struggle across the Med towards the promised land. It is not unusual for a ship to return after a three-week patrol and find herself duty destroyer with all leave suspended and at two hours' notice for steam, even before her crew has time for a run ashore.

I follow the traditional pattern and strike a bargain with one of the dghaisamen who becomes our personal, unofficial ferry, keeping himself available most of the time to back up the motor-cutter. Later, when things get back to normal, he will travel with us on some trips and become part of the furniture. He also gets rid of our gash each day. I like to believe it is fed to the pigs, but Robby is convinced that it is sold to poverty-stricken Maltese in the back alleys of Valletta. Like me he has a respect for these people and is annoyed by the snide remarks made by many of our colleagues.

Petty Officer Bold, for example, who openly admits that he has no time for 'Malts', or for that matter anyone born south of the Isle of Wight. There are plenty more like him on board who can be relied upon to think up derogatory names for non-Brits wherever they go. They seem determined to destroy relations between the locals and the Navy, and I put it down to ignorance in Bold's case. I can find no excuse for the attitude of the first lieutenant however. Along with many ex-patriot dignitaries that come on board he seems to regard the Maltese as an inferior race, fit only to do menial tasks, drive buses and taxis, work in the dockyard, or run errands for their 'superiors'.

'If the British should ever leave this bloody island,' declares Jimmy in one of his more bombastic moods, 'the whole place would sink without trace.'

The person who bears the brunt of the first lieutenant's bigotry is Leading Steward Caruana, an educated Maltese who speaks better English than many of the lads on the messdeck. All our officers except one treat Caruana and his stewards with respect, but Jimmy goes out of his way to keep them servile.

I ask the leading steward what he thinks would happen if the Navy ever left Malta and he thinks hard for a moment or so before saying quietly, 'It will be a hard time for a while. Especially for those who work in the dockyard or depend on the Navy for their livelihood. In fact I know the very thought of such a catastrophe scares the older ones. However, there are others, like myself, who find people like Bold and the first lieutenant hard to take. I think we would rather be poor and in charge of our own affairs – after all, there are few rich Maltese, and most of them are the ones who toady to the British and tell everyone else that we cannot live without them.'

'Yet you are willing to work for us. Serve the officers, and wear the uniform,' I accuse gently.

He smiles. 'Do you really think we have a choice? I have a brother in Italy who worked for the Germans: He had no choice either. In the end he stuck a knife into the back of one of his bosses. No, Swain. We do not sell our souls – only our labour.'

Old memories flood back as I stroll along Sliema waterfront. This is where I drank myself stupid after the *Avon* was bombed by the Luftwaffe. Over there under the shadow of the high cliffs of Valletta is the place where I took shelter while the bombing went on, and took advantage of a girl half crazy with fear, who wanted only to feel the security of someone's arms about her. A hot flush courses through my body for I am not too proud of that memory. A lot of blokes died that day while I was safely indulging myself. What a target those planes would find now with this huge fleet laid out in full array.

'Big-eats, navy!' invites a grinning, mahogany-faced boy, indicating the open doorway of a small cafe. I ignore him and walk on. I am looking for something better today; a secluded restaurant where the service is good and I have a real choice of food. Just up ahead there is a large hotel with an expensive menu on display outside. I walk in through heavy swing doors to be confronted by a mincing head-waiter.

'Sorry, sir. Officers only, I'm afraid.'

*

The boarding party go off to Ghain Tuffieha with Sub-Lieutenant Connault in command, backed up by two POs: one from the engineroom department, and the other Petty Officer Bold. I watch them rattle away in a couple of three-tonners and settle back to my daily harbour routine.

Despite being mid-winter the sun shines all day and the island shimmers with washed-out colour while interminable church bells toll away in the background. The men work bare-chested on the upper deck, and for once the cleaning of brass and washing down paintwork don't seem too much of a chore.

We have our share of defaulters who succumb to the seedy temptations of the Gut and Floriana and find themselves in trouble with authority on shore. Three of our stokers with skinfuls of local hooch find themselves in front of Government House as the local artillerymen are changing guard and decide to give the ceremony added zest by introducing commands of their own. The military are too well-drilled to be taken out of their stride however, and our lads are arrested by half a dozen local policemen who all seem to be ten feet tall with an inborn hatred for all things nautical. The stokers arrive back on board next day battered and bruised, to face further sanction from their first lieutenant.

I have warned everyone to stay clear of the local brew and drink 'Blue Label' beer if they must go on the piss. The colourless liquid that masquerades as booze is treated with great respect by the natives. It might look harmless but has a devastating effect on anyone not used to it. As far as Signalman Cummings is concerned it is the ideal mixture – cheap and lethal. Somehow he manages to stay out of my clutches, although everyone on board knows he has been on a perpetual binge since he finished his punishment. My policy is to let things ride so long as they remain unseen, and he is capable of doing his duty.

After six days we receive an urgent signal from the training camp informing us that things are not as they should be and there is a certain amount of concern amongst the senior Marine officers about the behaviour of our men. The captain decides to send the first lieutenant, a surgeon lieutenant from Bighi and myself to investigate. Complaints from Ghain Tuffieha usually come from disgruntled matelots who reckon they are being unfairly treated by their age-old antagonists, the Marines. Almost invariably these complaints are completely unfounded.

The Monday Mutiny

We are met by a major with a trim moustache, a wiry body and close-cropped hair when we are arrive at the gate. Who seems desperately anxious to explain what led to the signal being sent. He admits that the course is tough, but insists it needs to be, because they have to take thirty-odd over-fed, under-conditioned layabouts and turn them into fighting men who have to face up to some very determined resistance when they leap on to the deck of an immigrant ship.

'We have been told to toughen them up,' he says as we walk through the camp. 'Make them confident, so that they can jump from one moving ship to another whilst being tossed about, probably in the dark, while the immigrants turn steam hoses on them and hurl bottles, cans, iron bars, and any other missiles they can lay their hands on. Your men will have to keep their feelings under restraint and hold their fire under extreme provocation. They will find themselves isolated at times when they are surrounded by a mass of yelling immigrants determined to throw them back into the sea. There will be women too, with steel knitting needles and open scissors who know exactly where to hit or jab a man. So any thought of chivalry goes by the board.

'Believe me it is no picnic. The immigrants are learning new tricks every day. When the destroyers boarded the first ships they went into it blind. They were not sure how to go about it. Their efforts were unco-ordinated, and the sailors balked at hitting out at the women: it developed into a bloody brawl. The first sailors that went over were overwhelmed and HMS *Childers* actually sent over her hockey and cricket teams with bats and sticks to rescue their mates. The Jews were so tightly packed they could scramble across their shoulders to reach the bridge. When the ship arrived at Haifa both immigrants and boarding party were in a frightful mess. There was hardly a sailor without an injury, and the whole thing was a bloody fiasco which brought little credit to the Navy.

'That was why this course was devised. New methods

have been tried and tested. Platforms have been built out from the destroyers' bridges to make it easier to get a lot of men across in quick time. We are teaching sailors to wade into tear gas and fire crackers and make their way to pre-determined objectives such as the wheelhouse and engine-room.

'The Jews are learning too. They turned fuel hoses on to the deck of one destroyer, then tried to set fire to her. They dropped lifeboats on to the decks and damaged two destroyers so badly they are in dock now, under repair. They have installed emergency steering so that even when our men have taken the wheelhouse they still control the ship from below. On top of all that we have to pander to world opinion and try not to appear brutal. It is a difficult, dangerous job, Lieutenant,' he says to Jimmy, 'and we have only two weeks to train your men for it.'

'What is the problem with *Condor*'s sailors?'

The major stops and faces Jimmy squarely. 'Your petty officer is the real trouble. We try to engender a competitive spirit here; in fact we thrive on it, but he has taken it beyond all bounds, and he is running your men into the ground. I am told by my sergeants that they are out on the assault course during the dog watches training like mad. That may sound very commendable on the face of it, but when they turn up at first parade next morning they are tottering with exhaustion. We expect that for the first three days or so while they loosen up and get used to the unaccustomed exercise, but usually they begin actually to enjoy it after that. They should be taking things in their stride by now, but they are like a lot of old men, and it's all because of your petty officer.

'My sergeant is in a dilemma. He cannot ease off on the men, nor discourage enthusiasm, but he can see where this is leading and that all his efforts will come to nought unless something is done. I have had a word with your sub-lieutenant and PO Bold, but they seem to think I am being patronising.' He shrugs and moves on again. 'That's it in a nut-shell. I thought a word from you might put things back in order.'

'Where are they now?'

The major brightens. 'Ah, you've arrived at an opportune moment. They should be coming to the end of the assault course and starting practice jumps on to steel plates to get them used to landing correctly on the deck of a ship. If we hurry, we will catch them at it.'

He leads the way up a long slope strewn with sharp stones and boulders where the sun has bleached the ground into a white dust and only a few straggled clumps of scrub manage to survive.

Parties of helmeted men run and leap about, urged on by leathery-faced sergeants who scream abuse and encouragement at them when they falter. I get a whiff of tear-gas and look upwind to see a line of men descending into a long trench wearing respirators.

'Nah take orf yer mask and do it agin!' roars their instructor with a delighted grin, and they scramble through and out of the other side with their eyes streaming and coughing their innards out.

'We can't afford to have them panic if they are caught in a cloud of gas on the crowded deck of a ship,' explains the major in response to Jimmy's raised eyebrows.

At the top of the hill a low wall runs alongside a ditch to the empty shell of a ruined building. It is deserted and the major stops with a puzzled expression on his face.

'Strange,' he mutters, looking about. 'This is where they should be at this moment. Look, you can see the metal plates where they jump. We have turned it into a set course which includes several jumps and lends itself to competition amongst the participants.' He looks at his watch. 'If they were on schedule they should be here,' he repeats bewildered.

A sound drags our eyes towards the left in time to see a breathless sergeant running towards us. He snaps a salute and gathers breath to report. 'We have got a problem, sir.'

He glances anxiously at us as though he is reluctant to go on while we are listening.

'You can speak up, sergeant. What sort of problem?'

'Serious, sir. The whole thing has got out of 'and, and I think we might 'ave a dead man on our 'ands.'

'Good grief!'

The sergeant looks uncomfortable. 'He collapsed second time round the assault course, sir. One of the seamen is trying to revive 'im, and I've sent to base for a stretcher. It's bad, I'm afraid, sir.'

'Where is he?' asks the surgeon, breaking his silence and pulling the sergeant's eyes round. He is trying to sort out who we are and why we have suddenly appeared on his territory.

'It's all right, sergeant,' reassures the major. 'This is a doctor, and these people are from the men's ship.'

Still slightly bemused he leads us down a path and soon we see a small knot of anxious men gathered about a slumped seaman. Tanky and Leading Seaman Henry are tending him.

'Let me through!' snaps the surgeon abruptly, kneeling down beside the prone shape of one of our ODs. After a moment he looks up with a sigh. 'It is no good. The man's gone.'

'How did he die?' asks Jimmy coldly.

'I won't know until I have carried out a thorough examination, and there will be a post-mortem of course, but I'd guess he had a heart attack.'

The major's face is hard. He turns to his sergeant. 'You said something about a second time round? Since when did we put these men through the assault course twice in succession?'

The marine looks uncomfortable. 'The first run was sloppy. We decided it should be done again.'

'We?'

'The three of us, sir. The officer, the PO and me.'

'You are in serious trouble, sergeant,' the major rasps

harshly. 'You should know by now that you are in command and totally responsible for these men while they are under your instruction. You take orders from no one other than your own superiors; I don't care if he is a bloody admiral.'

'Sir.'

The major moderates his voice. 'I see the stretcher-party coming. You will march the others back to barracks immediately, and do not leave the camp until I have spoken to you.'

The sergeant pulls himself erect to snap a salute, but before he can turn to move away Jimmy barks, 'Stand fast!' and the sergeant freezes.

'I want an explanation here and now. What have you to say, Connault?'

Before Subby can reply the major jumps in. 'No, Lieutenant. We must do this correctly. March the men back, sergeant, then report to the guardroom.' With that he strides off, leaving us to follow.

I watch the pathetic bundle being placed on the stretcher then walk alongside the bearers as they carry the OD down to the sprawl of buildings. The shouts of marine instructors sound thin in the dry air now, and the heat has gone out of the sun. Far below the high cliffs I catch a glimpse of turquoise where the water in St Paul's Bay is so clear it is possible to see a ship's cable running out to an anchor.

I have no part in the interrogation that follows so I seek out the canteen and sit over a cup of strong tea. It is mid-afternoon and only a few off-duty marines are there. They glance up briefly when I enter, then return to their muttered conversations; all except one sergeant who strolls over to my table and studies my face for a moment before asking, 'Can I sit here?'

I nod and he rasps the opposite chair back and sits squarely in front of me.

'I hear your man's dead, Chief. I hope you ain't gonna blame it on Eddie. He's bin worried sick about the way things were going since that PO came. We've got our share of sadistic bastards, but that sod takes the biscuit. If you want a bit of free advice from one who has seen a lot of dabtoes come through 'ere. Don't take 'im on a boarding party. He is nothin –'

He is interrupted by one of *Condor*'s men coming in looking for me. 'The first lieutenant wants you, Swain.'

I find them in one of the classrooms. Jimmy, Subby and the major, all standing out in front of the desks while the sergeant lurks in one corner.

'Glad you could spare us a moment of your valuable time, Coxswain,' sneers Jimmy as I take my seat.

'Sorry, sir.'

He takes a step forward. 'We have to put this unfortunate incident behind us now. You have done well and the major is very impressed by your enthusiasm so let's keep it that way. It has been agreed it would not be right to carry on this afternoon, but we will make a fresh start in the morning. I think we can leave the programme to the marines and not try to break any records.' He turns to the major. 'Do you wish to add anything, major?'

The marine's face is deadly serious as he nods to his sergeant who barks everyone to attention as the officers file out. I am about to follow them, and get as far as the door when I notice Petty Officer Bold standing at the back of the room watching me with cold, calculating eyes. For a moment we stare hard at each other, and I swear there is a self-satisfied smirk on his lips.

On the way to Sliema Jimmy gives me instructions to go on to Bighi hospital and collect the few items of personal kit from the body. It is up to the parents to decide whether their son should have a full-blown naval funeral, or be flown home for a private interment. In the meantime, I must arrange for the usual auction sale of the man's effects so that his mess-mates can bid ridiculous prices, and donate the proceeds to his next of kin.

'Muir wasn't married then?' asks Jimmy.

The Monday Mutiny

'No, sir, he was only eighteen. Did the doctor say what he died of?'

'We won't know for certain until the results of the PM, but he thinks it was a heart attack.'

'Bit young for that wasn't he, sir?'

'The doctor says there is no age limit.' He looks sideways at me. 'Don't read more into it, Grant. You can forget any spurious suggestions put forward by Monday. I hope you will not allow any rumours to get about the ship.'

'No, sir.' I lapse into silence as the small truck rumbles along the dry, dusty road through sleeping villages where poverty stares out at us from black doorways and windows. We go by a small donkey being prodded along by its owner who watches our dust-cloud with brooding eyes until we round a bend and lose him. It is as though the sun has burnt the life out of the countryside.

*

'What's up with you?' Robby's growl shakes me out of my thoughts. 'You look like a cow with guts-ache, you miserable sod. I reckon you need a bloody good run ashore. Come on, let's act like a couple of wet-eared ODs and go dahn the Gut. We'll do the bars one by one all the way dahn and see if we can reach the bottom.'

'That's all Jimmy would need,' I snort. 'His coxswain and buffer returning from shore pissed out of their minds.' I grin at him. 'I could do with a few wets though, and I have yet to sample the dubious delights of Strait Street.' There is no reason I can see why the death of one matelot should affect me like this. It makes no sense at all. I should be able to shake it off, but it hangs over me like a cloud. It must be like Robby says; I need a bloody good run ashore to get it out of my system.

The Fleet gets paid every second Thursday and as this is the Friday after payday the streets are thronged with eager youngsters out to spend it all on one mad spree. On top of that two cruisers have arrived. One, an eight-inch County

Class on her way home with time-expired men, and the other a modern six-inch City Class with a company largely made up of fresh-faced kids out to prove they are 'Jack-me-hearty' types with well-rehearsed nautical rolls and silk dragons decorating their rolled-up cuffs.

It is a recipe for disaster and should not have happened. The plan was for the two ships to miss each other by several days, but a storm delayed the old County Class and fate finds them in port together. Now both crews come together in the seething canyon of debaucherie called the Gut, where the reverberation of numerous bands and self-styled Frank Sinatras bounce off the buildings that trap all sound and smell in the narrow street, turning it into a seething cauldron of concentrated licentiousness.

It is still early when Robby and I force our way through the mob past the 'Egyptian Queen', the 'New Life', and other dens of iniquity, until we find relative sanctuary in the 'Silver Horse' or – as more commonly known amongst its clientele – the 'Galvanised Donkey'. We have modified Robby's original idea of visiting every bar on the way down and settled for a much safer variation. Inside we turn away two girls who come to drink coloured water in return for a few favours underneath the table and sit back with our 'Blue Labels' to sample the atmosphere.

The noise from outside is subdued as yet, like the endless murmur of hungry zoo animals pacing cages as they wait for feeding time. In every bar matelots pour booze down their gullets and urge local talent to get on with the show. In the 'New Life' a wispy maiden called Sparrow will rise to the occasion after there has been a collection and squat over an empty bottle before ejecting it like a projectile with an expert squeeze of her muscles to the thunderous cheers of her drooling audience.

Elsewhere Minko and Johnny, two refugees from the stringent laws against homosexuality in England, will perform their Apache Dance in their own bar, and in every establishment things are building up towards a climax

The Monday Mutiny

when entertainment is taken out of the hands of the locals and the place explodes like a volcano.

Aloof from all this I am enthralled by a lady pianist who looks a cut above average as she plunks away at the keys. She has classic features, long limbs and a sophisticated air, and what's more, she is actually smiling at me. Obviously she has seen us chase away the local riff-raff and realises that I am not one of the rabble. I signal a waiter over and send a drink across. She holds it up and smiles even more invitingly. Is it possible I've latched on to the one quality woman in the area?

'Think you've cracked it, do yer?' Robby is chortling away as he watches my antics.

'Why not? She can see I'm no bloody half-hard OD. I'd say she is a cut above the rest.' I get annoyed when he chuckles even louder. 'What the hell's got into you, for Christ sake?'

Between gusts he spouts. 'Sorry, mate. I don't mean ter put yer down, but if yer puts yer 'and up her clouts you're in for a shock. Yer'll grab a 'andful of toggle-and-two – she's a bloke.'

'I'm hungry,' I declare, after a long silence. 'Come on, let's get some big-eats.'

Steak, egg and chips is the staple diet for matelots who frequent this place, and waiters are kept on the run during pay-week. It is as though there is a conveyor-belt serving the rear of every eating house for the pattern is identical. By the time we have consumed ours the animal sounds from outside are reaching a crescendo. The two ships' companies have located each other and the general hubbub is punctuated with shouts of 'Git yer knees brown' and 'Wait till yer sees the price of fags!'

The popular bars emit a bedlam of mind-bending noise, and the walls quake to the raucous blast of drunken reverie. Blurry-eyed sailors spill out into the alley to slush through pools of vomit and spilled beer as they stumble blindly in search of the next outrage. The trick is to find a safe corner

The Monday Mutiny

from where we can sit and observe this human zoo.

The patrols have not moved in yet. They know from long experience the exact moment to interfere, and by that time most of their victims should be too drunk to feel or complain about the treatment they receive. The miracle is that no one actually gets killed or badly maimed. Men fall from first floor windows, lie unconscious in the gutter while others walk over them, scratch and tear at each other as they roll about the filthy cobbles, and the uproar is tremendous.

Robby and I retire with a couple of bottles of whisky to a small doss-house where the beds are clean and a window looks out on the scene. We sit there engrossed as the authorities move in. The training camp could learn much about mob-handling from these experts. The police and naval patrolmen charge into the mêlée with truncheons drawn and coshes flaying at everything that moves. They are a moving tide of brown uniforms with white-gaitered patrolmen following up astern. Guilty and innocent alike are grabbed, punched, kicked, gouged and bludgeoned into submission, then taken to the rear where those judged to have assaulted the police – worked out on a percentage basis – are thrown into police vans, while others of milder disposition are arrested by their own kind.

The stench of vomit and stale beer clogs the atmosphere and still the reedy sounds of persevering musicians filter out above the moving battle. Men who are not directly involved who have somehow avoided the chaos move in behind the ebbing tide of violence to take their places at vacated tables to begin the whole process again.

Our host wakens us with glasses of tea. It is always served in a glass in these places, and heaven help anyone who doesn't take milk and sugar. We wallow in basins of cold water and dress quickly for we have to be back on board by eight o'clock. Outside the alley is filled with debris from last night's battle stagnating in the growing heat of the day. I don't feel too bright but I am positively blooming with health alongside some of the dilapidated wretches we see trying to come to terms with the dawn.

Robby and I keep conversation down to minimum and stay in the shadows, allowing the fresh morning air to evaporate the nauseous, mouth-clogging taste of our binge as we merge with a growing tide of dockyard workers. We find a solitary dghaisaman taking an early doze in Msida Creek and save ourselves a long trek round the waterfront. I get a whiff of nostalgia as he rows out past HMS *Wolfe* and I see one of her boats preparing for sea. The casing-party are stowing away mooring ropes and someone gives a couple of short toots on her siren to test it. I can visualise the quiet routine going on inside her as reports come in from all the compartments, then I turn away and shift her from my mind because memories like that can be painful.

On board *Condor* there is a general bustle of activity as the crew prepare for a new day. I find Jimmy in a filthy mood when we fall in for 'both watches', and Robby wilts under a string of complaints about the state of the upper deck. With many of the seamen away on the course it is difficult to maintain Jimmy's meticulous standards and he makes no concession for depleted man-power. I am glad to retreat to my office to sort out the day's paperwork, but I am hardly sat down before Monday interrupts with a polite knock at my door.

'Can't it wait?' I protest harshly.

'No, Swain; I don't think so. Cummings was put on report last night. He has been charged with being drunk and incapable whilst on duty.'

'Shit!' I bang the desk angrily. 'They'll throw the book at him for that, the bloody idiot!'

'It is worse than that. We found him in the passage outside of the pusser's store choking in his own vomit. I've got him down in the sick-bay now, and he is still only half-conscious. Apparently it was his birthday yesterday, and apart from knocking back sippers from almost everyone on the messdeck he has been drinking rot-gut smuggled from ashore. He is in a hell of a state and I think he should go to hospital.'

'Oh no, not that again!'

'I tell you he is a sick man, Swain. He is not fit to carry on. He can't live without booze now and it is killing him. His mates think they're doing him a favour by playing along with his stupidity, and now he has taken to going through a whole ritual of travelling in the London Underground: strap-hanging from the hammock rails, the lot. It is quite a performance. There is nothing left for him now, Swain. His mind is gone. Unless something is done he could kill himself.'

'For Christ's sake!' I chaff at him. 'That bloody business with the underground is an old game. Lots of blokes pretend to ride in the rush-hour; it's a sort of nostalgic prank. I have known Cummings longer than you, Monday, and I've seen others like him. They go through these periods, but it passes, and then there are long spells when they are fine. If he was drunk on watch he'll get his punishment. Seven days on bread and water should straighten him up.'

'Or kill him,' snorts Monday aggressively. 'Jimmy talked me out of going to the skipper last time, but I'm not going through that farce again. If necessary I will refuse to carry out my duties until someone takes notice of what I've got to say.'

'Now look here, lad,' I stand up fuming. 'This is the Royal Navy. You don't make threats like that and get away with it. You had better simmer down before you find yourself in trouble.'

His shoulders droop in despair. 'Well, what else am I supposed to do? I like to think I am a professional man, yet no one will take my advice.'

'Forget it, Monday. The Navy has been looking after its own for generations. Cummings will get chokey for this, and that will mean an automatic medical inspection, so it is out of your hands. Now, get out of here and let me get on.'

The Monday Mutiny

He seems to slump even more and goes on resignedly, 'All right, you win, Swain. I can't buck the system. While I'm here though I had better report two cases of gonorrhoea.'

I sit down. 'Well, they'll see the quack, and once he's confirmed it they'll go ashore for treatment and get twenty-one days' stoppage of leave – that's standard procedure.'

He sniggers bitterly. 'Bloody marvellous, isn't it? Catch the boat up and there's a ready-made formula, but God help some poor bastard who gets hooked on booze.'

I'm getting sick of all this. 'Look, Monday. We have all got our problems, and we have all got our own ideas of how things should be done. Fortunately the Navy isn't a bloody democracy or the whole thing would fall apart. Do like the rest of us; get on with your job, do as you're told and you can't go far wrong.'

He shrugs hopelessly before turning to go. I feel a twinge of sympathy for him but nothing is perfect in this world, and the sooner he finds that out the better.

*

Time is a good healer. Ten days later we are sliding out to sea and Cummings has done his chokey. Monday is confounded by the signalman's resilience when he returns to the ship looking as healthy and ebullient as ever. It doesn't surprise me, for there are hundreds of Cummingses in the service with leather-lined stomachs and iron constitutions. I just curse the way I laid myself wide open to Jimmy's scorn for the second time when I reported Monday's concern again.

'You want to watch yourself, Coxswain,' he advises sardonically. 'You are turning into a wet nurse for that skate.'

The skipper clears lower deck for one of his rare pep-talks and tells us we are heading for the Straits of Messina.

'It should be a pleasant interlude, and we will take full

advantage of it to carry out evolutions. We are looking for a forty-five foot, steel-hulled motor-cruiser with cabins fore and aft and a small cockpit amidships. Last seen she was painted white with red boot-toppings. She may look innocent enough, but we have reason to believe she is carrying arms and explosives for the Irgun.

'In case you do not know about the Irgun, I can tell you it is a radical organisation dedicated to using force to gain their aims. They are led by a man called Manachin Begin, and they are extremely ruthless. It was they who admitted blowing up the King David Hotel and killing at least ninety people, so be warned. We are dealing with dangerous terrorists.'

He changes his stance and a more pleasant look transforms his features as he goes on. 'In the meantime we will be working the ship up to full efficiency, starting this afternoon when a target-towing aircraft will rendezvous and give our gunners a chance to display their skills. Petty Officer Bold tells me his four-inch can achieve eighteen rounds a minute. If they do, and they get their rounds somewhere near the target, I will be impressed enough to think about awarding an extra make and mend when we reach port.' He turns to Jimmy. 'That's all, Number One. Make certain the look-outs know their jobs.'

He leaves behind a silence when he goes. Each man working his mind over the words, trying to reason them out so that their meaning is clear. When they are dismissed the talk centres on Jews and Arabs while we wait for the target to arrive.

The shoot brings relief for there is a satisfying simplicity about loading a gun, aiming it at a spot slightly ahead of a moving wind-sock so that shell and target reach the same spot at the same time. Once the gunners acquire their rhythm the barrels belch flame and noise at regular intervals, and the acrid tang of burnt cordite mingles with the stale smell of sweat as loading numbers run with their charges. This is what they are familiar with, what they are drilled for, and the complications of Israel can be pushed aside while they pock-mark the sky with shrapnel. With keen anticipation we tense up and wait for the order to 'open fire'.

'All guns follow director – A gun, with HE, load load load!' I can hear the range-setters repeating the orders from the gunnery control officer.

'Stand to aircraft starboard!' Robby will have the drogue in his sights now, moving his joystick control expertly while every gunlayer follows every move on their indicators.

'Check check check! Cease fire! All guns train fore and aft!'

Now what? I strain my ears. Maybe the drogue has come adrift even before the shoot starts. The wheelhouse door slides open and one of the oerlikon gunners pokes his head in. 'I've bin sent to relieve you, Swain. You are wanted on the bridge.'

Before he stops panting confirmation comes down the voicepipe. The ship is wallowing to a long swell when I go out to mount the ladder, and when I reach the bridge everyone is staring upward. I follow their stares and see they are not looking at the target aircraft which is droning forlornly down our port side, but at the mast. Above the sound of wind and sea a wild voice is chanting.

'Blessed is everyone that fearest the Lord; that walketh in his ways. For thou shalt eat the labour of thine hands!'

High on the truck of the mast Cummings stands with his hair blowing in the wind, holding on with one hand and brandishing an inflated condom with the other. Now he breaks into song.

'Orl the boys in the messdeck dropped their buckets and said fuck it, when they 'eard that the buffer 'ad kicked the fuckin' bucket.'

We hold our breath as he swings out with the roll of the ship, laughing down into our upturned faces.

'You sent for me, sir?' Monday is standing at my side, bare-headed as he reports to Jimmy.

The Monday Mutiny

The captain thrusts his way through the throng to interject. 'I'm told you know about this man, Monday. What do you suggest we do now?'

Before he can answer a loud whoop comes from the masthead. 'Full fathom five thy father lies. Of his bones are coral made; seanympths hourly ring 'is bell – hark now I hear them – ding-bloody-dingdong-bell!'

'Silence!' screams Jimmy when one of the signalmen sniggers, and the aircraft roars disconsolately down our starboard side.

'Yeoman!' calls the skipper. 'Thank the pilot. Express my regrets, and tell him his services are no longer required.' He turns to us and growls. 'I want this bloody nonsense concluded before Cummings kills himself. Is it possible to talk that idiot down from his perch?'

Everyone is looking at Monday and he shakes his head. 'I suffer from vertigo, sir. I couldn't climb up there.'

'You don't need to. Surely you can speak to him from the director?' sneers the first lieutenant.

'That would be dangerous, sir,' insists Monday, ignoring Jimmy and speaking directly to the skipper. 'I think Cummings is in a world of his own. It would be like waking a sleepwalker. He might do anything if he is suddenly startled. Someone will have to get close enough to talk quietly to him. Gain his confidence and try to find out where he is in his mind. Once we do that we can play his game and hopefully coax him down, or at least get close enough to grab him. I would make a mess of it because I would panic half-way up.' I admire his honesty. There is no reason why a sickberth attendant should be able or willing to climb masts, but it still takes guts to admit it. I suddenly realise all eyes are focused on me.

'It will have to be you then, Coxswain,' says Jimmy.

Monday coughs apologetically. 'No, sir. Not him either, I'm afraid. You see, Cummings sees him as an enemy.'

'I reckon I know the bloke,' suggests the yeoman, and because we all respect him we hang on his words. 'His best

The Monday Mutiny

mate is Sparks Wilson. If anyone can get through to Cummings, he can.'

The captain sighs heavily, sick of the whole thing. 'Do whatever you think best; but for God's sake get on with it.'

'For the lips of a strange woman drop as a honeycomb, and her mouth is smoother than oil.' The signalman's in full spate now, preaching to the sea of upturned faces and pointing an accusing finger into thin air. 'But her end is bitter as wormwood; sharp as a two-edged sword – her feet go down to death; her steps take hold on Hell!'

'Listen to that bible-punchin' bastard!' growls someone.

'Makes sense to me,' says the yeoman. 'Maybe he is more sober than he looks.'

'Silence!' shouts Jimmy again, as Wilson arrives on the scene.

He leans back to stare up at his mate for a moment. 'Pillock!' he snarls. 'If he touches that live aerial no one will need ter worry.' He goes over and withdraws the red transmitting board that breaks the circuit to the big antennas. No telegraphist nor radar-man would neglect to remove the board before going up amongst the electronics.

'A norse! A norse! My kingdom for a norse!'

'Bring the ship upwind, pilot,' orders the skipper tightmouthed. 'At least we can ease the roll. Slow ahead together.' He deliberately turns his back on Jimmy and goes on, 'Well, Number One. How much longer do I have to wait?'

'It's a delicate position, sir.'

The skipper doesn't answer, but his silence speaks volumes.

Cummings has lowered himself to straddle the yard with his short legs dangling either side. He seems to be staring at something.

'Maybe we could coax 'im down wiv 'is tot, sir.'

'No!' interposes Monday. 'Booze is poison to him.'

One of the bridge telephones whines plaintively. 'It's for you, sir.' One of the bridge messengers hands the set to

The Monday Mutiny

Jimmy. 'It's the duty engineer.'

We watch in silence while he listens with the phone held firm against his ear. 'Thank you,' he breathes, and replaces the handset with slow deliberation.

'Blast!' he explodes, looking at the skipper. 'Report from below, sir. They have found the remains of a boat's compass. All the alcohol is drained from the bowl.'

The captain bangs a fist hard on the bridge-rail. It is the first time I've seen him lose his cool. We follow his gaze as he lifts his head to see Cummings pointing a wavering arm at something he sees at the end of the yardarm.

'Gerroff, you old bastard – you're not my father!'

'I've had enough of this,' snaps Jimmy. 'Cummings!' His voice carries the whole length of the ship and the gun crews stare back with blank faces before switching up again.

Cummings is frozen with his arm outstretched as the first lieutenant's shout drills into him. I can see him fighting to drive away his visions.

'Cummings!' blasts Jimmy again. 'Come down at once!'

Monday sucks in his breath. It is too late to stop the first lieutenant and we hold our breath as the signalman slowly bends his head to stare down. His vacant eyes pick out Jimmy and a look of bestial hatred transforms his face.

'You – you two-ringed bastard!' He straightens his legs until he is pressed back against the mast. Suddenly he shrieks with maniacal laughter; pointing downwards. 'I've always wanted ter piss on yer from a great height, you sod!'

He is fumbling with his buttons and we dive for cover as he waves his penis about, spraying the bridge with urine.

That does it; I find myself inside the trellis-work of the mast; hidden beneath the black box that serves as a crow's-nest. A man could climb up on the steel ladder inside the framework and stay hidden almost to the top ...

'Wilson!' I call in a hoarse whisper.

'What?'

'You reckon he'll come down for his tot?'

' 'E'd walk on water for 'is tot.'

'Right, then nip below and tell ERA Foreman to give you his medicine bottle – tell him I'll make up for it later.' As Sparks clatters away I glance at Jimmy and see him glaring back at me. For a moment I think he is going to give me a blast for condoning the bottling of rum, but he thinks better of it and looks away to concentrate like the rest of us on the lonely figure who seems to be quiet now. He is leaning back on the mast, his wild eyes searching our faces. The malice has gone from him, and he looks utterly alone up there.

'I think I could go up inside the mast.' I jerk round at Monday's quiet voice. He is sweating and his mouth is tight as he looks up through the latticework with the sun burning a black shadow across his face.

'Wilson is going to have a crack at it.'

'That's no good, Swain. Wilson might get him started down but he may not be able to sustain his persuasion all the way. Just one false move could mean disaster. Cummings is a broken man, Swain. The booze is eating out his brain.'

I glance at Jimmy who nods grudgingly.

'I want absolute silence.' Monday looks meaningfully at Jimmy, who chokes back his outrage with great difficulty.

'Get on with it, man!' he growls. 'We can't stand round waiting all day. We'll keep silent.'

'Just take it easy, I'm right behind you,' I assure him.

Monday climbs the ladder slowly, testing every rung as he goes and never looking down. There is a small hatch cut into the rear of the metal box and up to that point the going is easy. The leading SBA stays partly hidden against the side of the box, with the heavy corner-strut of the trellis mast between him and Cummings. From here one can see the whole length of the ship and the gaping mouth of the funnel with a thin haze of exhaust streaming aft. Now he must climb to the outside of the mast so that he is no longer encased inside the framework with its false sense of security.

We watch anxiously as he stretches to grasp the warm

steel and pulls his body up to the rim of the box, wriggling his body out past the metal strut to search for a foothold on the ladder with nothing beneath him but a sheer drop to the deck. He holds his face hard against the ladder; not daring to lean out to make it easier to work into a good position. He works blind, fiddling with his shoe to find a rung as he scrambles awkwardly with sweat dripping from his face. His progress is agonisingly slow and I have to bottle my patience as he moves like a sloth towards the truck. The back of his shirt is black with sweat and I can see his limbs shaking from here. He has to stop for a moment with his body moulded against the ladder and I can almost smell his fear.

Cummings is sobbing quietly now. Rolling his head about as though in pain. His body slumps, going limp as everything drains and his muscles turn to rubber. The slightest movement of the ship sets him swaying for he has no will to hold on, and he is content to allow the ship to take charge.

Monday is close up to the framework of the truck where the mainmast ends and both yards stretch out either side. Until this moment he has been partly concealed by the metalwork, but now he must ease his body right onto the truck in full view of the signalman should Cummings choose to turn round. There is only a foot or so between them both but he cannot reach out to grasp Cummings until he is sitting on the truck. With infinite caution he drags his backside up on to the ledge. Now, all he has to do is reach out, grab hold, and hang on until someone can come to help. I am already close up against the crow's-nest, ready and tensed, waiting for the exact moment to scramble up.

Monday is gritting his teeth and stretching an arm out towards the signalman and I am poised ready to back him up. We almost have him when the safety valve blasts open with an excruciating roar. I grip white-knuckled and engulfed in the thick, hot, suffocating cloud of steam that seems to go on forever. I am oblivious to everything but the awful noise and in my mind I see the effect it has on Cummings. I see him spiralling out and falling to the steel deck far below, for surely this must be the final shock to send him off his rocker?

The noise shuts off suddenly to leave a stunned silence. My brain is numb and my clothing soaked with evaporated steam. I hear someone clambering up from below and look down to see Wilson and the yeoman on their way up to help. I look down past them, expecting to see the spreadeagled body of Cummings splayed out on the deck.

There is nothing there. Perhaps he has gone over the side. I close my eyes. Too late to do anything about him now I raise my eyes and stare into the remaining swirl of spent steam. It is thinning out to reveal two vague, shadowy figures silhouetted against the sky. One is crouched terrified against the mast, frozen and unable to move. The other has arms outstretched over him like some old world prophet.

'My hour is almost come, when I to sulphurous and tormenting flames must render myself!'

'Stow that stupid nonsense, Cummings,' I bark angrily. I am no longer concerned if he jumps or not. That jibbering besotted idiot is no use to anyone and all my concern is for Monday who seems to have gone to pieces as he stares at me with pleading eyes.

'I can't move, Swain. I was all right coming up but I can't climb down.' He is panting, wide-eyed and sweating.

'Don't worry, lad,' I assure him. 'Hang on a moment more while we haul up some tackle with one of the halliards. We'll lower you down in a bos'n's chair. Just keep your eyes shut until you reach the deck.'

He is trembling violently when we strap him in, and almost stops breathing when we hoist him out clear to lower him down. I don't think I've ever seen anyone so terrified in my life, and he falls into the waiting arms of the blokes on the signal-deck like a limp rag-doll.

The Monday Mutiny

Now for the other one. Cummings is burbling away to himself with saliva dribbling from his lips. It sounds like he is talking to his father again; slobbering over us as we strap him into the chair and send him down. The yeoman and I lead him through the messdeck. I must have missed the pipe to stand down from action stations for most of the men are there, trying to avert their eyes as we drag our burbling bundle towards the sickbay.

Inside Monday is waiting, and he says nothing while we help him put the signalman into one of the lower cots with the safety rail lifted to stop him rolling out. That done I turn to Monday who deliberately turns away to busy himself in one corner, waiting for us to leave.

'Monday!'

'Leave it, Swain,' he says in a thick voice.

'It took a lot of guts to do what you did.'

He makes no reply, just persists in folding and refolding a sheet. I feel I can't leave it like that. The poor bastard looks as though he is tearing himself apart. 'I'm telling you, everyone in the ship knows what it cost you to climb that ladder. You've got nothing to be ashamed about.'

'Ashamed!' I jump back as he swings on me with his eyes blazing. 'Ashamed! Do you think I give a shit what those morons think? Jesus Christ, Chief! I told both you and Jimmy what could happen and you bloody-well ignored me. The whole crew watched me fall to pieces up there and you say I've got nothing to be ashamed about. Don't tell me that – tell them!' He flings the words at me. 'What's so fucking terrible about a bloke who can't swing round the rigging like a sodding monkey? You ignored my warnings and allowed Cummings to come close to killing himself and you think I should apologise for my vertigo. You make me bloody sick.'

'All right, Monday. That's enough. You've had a bad time so I'll ignore your insubordination, but you've got it wrong. Cummings got hold of some neat alcohol. He was crazy with booze, but he brought it on himself.'

'Did he now. Well just for your information, Swain: he needs a stomach pump and I haven't got one. I can try to make him vomit some of that poison out of his system before it burns his insides, but he should be in hospital, and he should be seen by a doctor. We are not out of the woods yet, not by a long chalk.'

'All right. I will report that to the skipper at once. We might be able to transfer him to another ship with a doctor. Meanwhile you'll just have to do your best.'

Outside in the messdeck the men were settling down and a sudden gust of laughter drags my eyes towards the bulkhead door that leads out to the seamen's bathroom. 'Nancy' Norman, one of the quartermasters, is doing his party piece. He is a big man, but soft-skinned and podgy, who pretends to be queer. To my mind he pretends so hard he is almost there. Right now he is performing his favourite trick by tucking his genitals between his thighs so that from the front he looks like a woman. He has the knack of holding them there while he minces through the ship to the roar of applause. The climax comes when he reaches his own mess and bends over to display his round buttocks with the end of his old man peeking out. Today I can see nothing amusing and draw a roar of protest when I put a stop to his antics.

Four

We manage to ship Cummings on a homeward-bound Hunt Class destroyer. Strapped into a Robinson stretcher he is ferried across in our cutter, and with a farewell toot she is gone, leaving us to continue our journey to the straits, where we take station between sun-soaked cliffs with white-housed villages spilling down to the sea. Within twenty-four hours the locals know our routine and bum-boats swarm round us each evening when we heave to for 'Hands to bathe'.

Fresh fruit, vegetables and fish are exchanged for soap, cigarettes and other commodities in short supply on shore. I keep an official eye over proceedings, but like the officers ignore anything but the most blatant breaches of the law, and we become firm friends with the Italians.

A straggling procession of merchant ships goes by, dipping their ensigns respectfully to us, while dozens of colourful fishing-boats putter past with their dark-skinned crews grinning white teeth at us as they prepare their nets. People pay large sums of money for cruises like this and it is difficult to concentrate on the reason for our presence here. Working on the upper deck is pleasant and the seamen are cultivating mahogany tans.

'I never thought I would spend my time swannin' up and dahn like this lookin' fer a poxy rich man's floatin' knockin' shop,' growls Robby as we lean on the guardrails watching swimmers cavorting in the crystal clear sea. 'What's it all abaht anyway?'

I'm too lazy to come to grips with that one. 'Christ knows! I doubt the bloody thing will come our way. Let's face it, would you chance it with a bloody great warship patrolling the channel?'

'Well what are we doin' 'ere then?'

'Blocking the way, of course. With us here they will have to find some other route.' I lean back and pat his shoulder. 'You stay here and work it all out. I've got some paperwork to do.'

My cabin is quiet and cool, and I saved my tot for a moment like this, when I can sit back and savour it. The door suddenly jumps open, jolting me upright; caught with the half-empty glass in my hand as Lieutenant Border peers in. He ignores the rum.

'We will have to change the watch-bill now that Cummings has left the ship, Coxswain. I have spoken to the first lieutenant and he has agreed to an extra SDO messenger to ease the strain on the signalmen until we can get a replacement.'

The cool atmosphere has sharpened my mind. Before he leaves I have to ask. 'This patrol doesn't make sense to some of the lads, sir. What is it all about? I know what the captain said, but a couple of MLs could have done this more efficiently.'

He hesitates for a moment before shutting the door quietly. There isn't much room in here for both of us as he leans against the bulkhead to study me seriously. 'How much do you know about the Jews and Israel, Grant?'

I ponder for a moment. 'Only that someone agreed in 1917 that they should have a land of their own in Palestine, but I have never been able to work out what happens to the Arabs.'

He sighs. 'I could talk for a month and neither of us would come out any the wiser. I have a friend who is Jewish, and before we sailed I asked him about it. He told me we must realise that the Jews regard themselves as one of the great historical races who have a divine right to a country of their own in Palestine, even though most of them have never been near the place, and would never have thought of going there had it not been for the events that have taken place since the War. Many of the people our lads will be asked to stop from reaching Israel are from horror camps. When they were released after the war ended they set off for homes they left in places like Poland only to find their houses occupied and anti-semitism as rife as ever. In fact they were often told that what Hitler had started the authorities would finish.

'They were hounded and abused, tortured and murdered until they fled back to the very camps where they had been interned and became "Displaced Persons", for whom no one wanted to become responsible.

'They found they were a nation without a country, and there is no dignity in that. They grew impatient with politicians who seemed to argue incessantly without achieving anything. They were getting stronger, taking up trades in their camp ghettos, and soon they began to look eastwards, remembering promises made about a land of their own. Those with education spoke of the "Balfour Declaration"; an ambiguously worded document that promised everything to everybody – a land for the Jews and guarantees for Arabs.

'An organisation was born called Hagana who began to arrange for immigrant ships to take people back to Palestine to build a new home, and the Arabs watched them coming; saw that they were not coming in ones, twos, tens or hundreds, but by the thousand, and that they were not intending merely to integrate with the indigenous people, but to take over and run the place. Introduce their own laws and govern, while the locals would benefit from their industry and expertise when they turned the desert into arable land, regardless of centuries of tradition and culture.'

He sighs dejectedly, looking down at the deck. 'We have to try to stem an overwhelming flood of immigrants and prevent a bloodbath. It is a mess, and quite frankly the first lieutenant is probably right when he says we should close our minds to the implications and just get on with our job. It isn't as simple as fighting the Germans, and I just wish I had a mind that didn't search for causes and values. It's an old cliché, Grant: "Ours is but to do or die etc". The snag is that in Nuremburg many Nazis will be pleading just that – they were not there to argue, but to carry out their duty.'

'Clear the water!' The pipe echoes through the ship as the swimming session comes to an end. Soon we will be plodding up and down again, but right now our conversation is interrupted, and I can see he is slightly embarrassed at voicing his inner thoughts like this. He must have kept it all bottled up for a long time, for it had little to do with the simple question I asked, and now he slides into the passage as half-naked matelots tumbled past smelling of the ocean and dripping all over the place. I feel the vibration building as the screws begin to rotate, and hear the sea singing past the hull.

'Cooks to the galley! Hands to clean!'

Routine is taking over once more as the messdeck fills with a babble of relaxed noise. I slide my door shut and resume my work.

*

During the middle watch I am called from my hammock to report to the bridge where I find the skipper and Border staring out into the night. There is no moon but the sky is studded with stars, and lights twinkle from the black loom of the land. Radar has picked up a contact. A miniscule dot that is moving out from the northern shore just west of Melito, and bearing down towards us. At first it is just one of a whole host of echoes, and all that sets it apart from the others is the way she holds her course and carries no running lights. Just a faint glow from the cabin shows as she approaches. The radar operator reckons she is about the right size for the boat we are looking for, and she is acting strangely enough to warrant investigation, for she is coming straight at us as though we do not exist.

The skipper was called from his bunk half an hour ago and the duty watch are standing by the cutter armed and ready to board. I am needed on the wheel in case we have to do some fancy manoeuvering, and as I climb down the starboard ladder I can see the dark shapes of the boarding party being inspected by Subby, and that the cutter is already turned out ready for lowering.

Inside the wheelhouse I relieve the quartermaster who takes over one of the telegraphs, leaving one man spare. I tell him to keep an eye on what goes on and try to give me a running commentary, for one of my failings is that I cannot keep my mind on my own affairs for long if I think I am missing something.

'Stop both!'

The ship loses way until we are slopping quietly on the small swell. I can hear Jimmy's harsh voice shouting orders for lowering the cutter, and the sharp 'clunk' as Dodger knocks off the slip to drop her into the drink with a hefty splash. Now the boarding party will be sliding down the lifelines and settling into their positions on the thwarts while Subby scrambles aft to take his place beside the coxswain. The engine stutters into its rhythm as Dodger takes her out in a wide sweep towards the cruiser. So far there has been no sign of life, nor any response to Border's shouts through a megaphone. Our twenty-one inch lamp bathes the small white boat in its glare, but the windows of her cabin remain blank and she plods on persistently.

'Ole Dodger's alongside now, Swain,' informs my lookout in a piping voice. 'Someone's gettin' ready to jump over to her. There ain't no sign of no one.'

My inside churns as a sudden surge of alarm courses through me. The skipper had talked about explosives and ammunition, but I am not the only one gripped with anxiety for the lad tells me the cutter is pulling back and leaving Subby and one other man on board the cruiser.

The Monday Mutiny

Like me they will be thinking about booby traps and testing everything before making a move. I leave the wheel and my principles behind for a moment to go and look for myself. It is hardly likely the ship will move until the cutter returns, and I am only two steps away from the wheel and voicepipe. I must see what is going on.

'What's happening now?' I ask, and the youngster jumps as my voice comes close to his left ear.

'Nothing much, Swain,' he replies when he's recovered. 'The cutter is lyin' off but I can't tell what Subby and his mate are doin'.'

I peer over his shoulder, conscious that I have left my post, but overwhelmed with curiosity. The two boats look ghostly in the white light as they sit in a black pool. The cutter is moving again now and when the boats come together there is a welter of activity.

They seem to be passing a heavy bundle across from the cruiser and an aldis lamp starts to flash a signal, then settles into a series of answering blinks in response to our bigger lamp. The cutter sweeps away from the cruiser to head back towards the quarterdeck.

I've pushed my luck far enough, and am setting the others a bad example, so reluctantly I return to the wheel and wait, trying to control my curiosity. It is a remarkably still night and the putter of the boat's engine carries easily to me, making it even more frustrating to stand quietly with the useless wheel in my hands, trying to sort out the vague sounds. My young lookout is not much help either, for he keeps saying he can't see anything, and when he does he misinterprets it. I am just at the point of having a go at him for being stupid when he flattens me with one bald statement.

'They're bringin' a body on board, Swain.'

'Stand by main engines!' The order jerks me back to my duty and the two telegraphs ring the message down to the engineroom. Looking quickly through the port on front I can see Robby and some men working on the fo'c'sle with steam rising from the winch. The cutter's falls will be led through snatch-blocks and on to the drums ready for hoisting her out of the water. I can hear Border giving orders.

'Take the strain!' The boat must be hooked on. 'Forward falls hoist!' That will bring her level. 'Hoist away!' Now she will be lifting out with her bilges dripping.

Other ships would have turned the whole crew out for this, manning the falls by hand, marrying them and stamping them along the deck. We do it the easy way and many of the watch below will wake up in the morning ignorant of all these goings on, but fresh to take up their duties.

'First lieutenant wants to know what about the cruiser, sir!' Someone is shouting up from just outside the wheelhouse and I don't hear the reply.

'Slow ahead together! Wheel amidships!' The vibrations come as she picks up speed. 'Starboard twenty!' I spin the spokes and feel her list slightly. There are feet clattering up the ladder leading up to the bridge and I imagine the cutter turned in and gripped hard against the pads. The boarding party will be returning their weapons, and that will be Border's feet ringing on the metal rungs as he goes up to report all secure to the skipper.

'Midships – Meet her – Steer zero nine zero!' I glance up when I have her settled on course and there, dead ahead, is the small cutter, wallowing as our bows move in towards her. The skipper is not going to recover her, and if we leave her she will become a navigational hazard, so this is the best way to sink her. Gunfire would only rouse the natives and although the boarding party will have opened her valves there is no guarantee she will sink. I lose sight of her as she goes under the keel, but I hear her breaking up as she rolls down the length of the ship. All that anyone will find now is a floating mass of wreckage that should disperse before morning.

*

The Monday Mutiny

'Coxswain!' the voicepipe yells in my ear.

'Sir?'

'You can stand down now. Thank you!'

'Aye aye, sir.' I turn the wheel over to the quartermaster and climb slowly down into the ship. All is quiet on the maindeck for it is three-thirty in the middle watch and soon the morning watch men will be called, so I tread lightly as I move aft to the sickbay. Monday is there on his own, looking as though he is preparing to turn in as he fiddles with a blanket on one of the bunks.

'What's the problem?' he asks abruptly, as though he resents my intrusion.

'Curiosity,' I say bluntly. 'A body was brought on board. Anyone I know?'

'You'll find out tomorrow. We are taking him back to Malta for an autopsy. We will be earning ourselves a reputation at Bighi Hospital.' He turns his eyes away.

'It's someone I know then; you would have said "no" otherwise.'

He looks up again. 'Can't you wait until morning? We have put him in the tiller-flat where he can remain undisturbed.'

'Where no one will see him, you mean.'

'Have it your way.'

'I think I know who it is.'

'You may be right, but I've bin told to keep my mouth shut.'

I nod slowly. 'Okay, Monday. You get turned in.' I turn to move out but find his hand suddenly on my shoulder.

'I've got to go aft with these blankets to cover him up decently – I could do with a hand.' He takes up a couple of folded blankets and faces me.

'Okay,' I say again, searching the shadowed lines of his face. 'I'll come along to help.'

He drops his eyes as I open the door for him. The whole ship seems to be sleeping, and out on the quarterdeck there is a purposeful throb to her screws with the wake pushing out either side as we thrust along at a good speed. The hatch leading down into the steering compartment is small and heavy, requiring a counterweight to make it easier to open. Inside a steel ladder clings to the forward bulkhead and I go down first.

Every sound is magnified down here and the vibration of the propellers make our feet dance on the deck. It is an echo chamber, resounding to the sound of the sea and the spinning shafts. Softer noises of hydraulics respond to the wheel as the quartermaster keeps her on course. If ever the other two steering positions were out of action this is where the ship would have to be conned. A hand-pump is situated on the forward bulkhead, and with the correct valves opened the rudder can be pumped round. It is a cumbersome task, made even more difficult because every order has to be relayed from the bridge, but we have practised it and in an emergency it would work.

Right now though everything is in order and the big tiller moves easily to every whim of the helmsman. The only thing out of place down here is the body stretched out on a canvas sheet; face up, with a calm, composed expression. The only sign of violence is a small, neat hole in the centre of Seddon's forehead.

'He will be away from his missus a damn sight longer than two and a half years now,' sneers Monday as he covers the body.

I ignore his sarcasm. 'Is that all there was on the boat?'

He straightens up, still staring at the body. 'There was a note pinned to the body.'

'Oh?'

'About twenty or so names and a message that said something about martyrs whose blood was on the hands of the British. It went on a bit, but that's all I could read before it was taken from me.' He looks at me. 'I think we can guess most of the rest.'

'Reprisals,' I grunt.

'What else? Seddon was a spy in their eyes. The skipper

reckons they deliberately leaked the information about the cruiser to keep at least one ship tied up, and to take reprisals, as you say.'

'Bastards!'

'Depends which side you're on, doesn't it, Swain?'

'As I said before, Monday. You think too much.' I climb the ladder, dragging my body out into the warm, fresh air. The ship is plunging into a head sea, and half a gale is tugging at the gun-cover of the after four-inch. I taste the acrid tang of funnel smoke swept aft by the wind, and there is a soulful whine far up in the rigging. The watch on deck shelters behind the 'midships Bofors sponson, sipping mugs of glutinous kye. Already the morning watch is being called and I pass several shadowy figures on their way up to relieve their mates.

There is no sleep for me this night. My hammock feels hot and sweaty and all the sounds I usually take for granted become intolerable. The ship is lively now, corkscrewing through the growing swells so that I swing in unison with my messmates, and the nearest police-light invades my small sanctuary with every second roll. My mind is over-active and churns over and over with conflicting thoughts that refuse to go away, and I'm grateful when the first rays of dawn shine through the scuttles.

Monday worries me. He goes about the ship wearing a dour, hangdog expression with hardly a word for anyone, and when he does condescend to speak he seems determined to steer the conversation in one direction. I tell myself not to over-react, and that the men will be unaffected: after all, show me a matelot who hasn't got something to gripe about. Yet somehow this is different and I wonder if it has reached the point when I should report my feelings to the first lieutenant. Perhaps if our relationship was as it should be I could have a quiet word with him without the need for it to go any further, but I know he will not compromise. He will either tell me not to bother him, or much worse, take action that could lead to a

The Monday Mutiny

confrontation with Monday. If that happens I have a feeling Monday will land himself in trouble.

Sliema Creek is almost empty when we reach Malta, and we find ourselves at 'stand-by' when we moor to head and stern buoys, with a Bay Class frigate duty ship, steamed up and ready to sail. We grant leave to one watch, but only until twenty-two hundred hours, and libertymen are warned not to stray from the immediate vicinity and to be available for recall at a moment's notice. It is a compromise, worked out to give at least one watch a run ashore.

In fact they do not even get off the ship for by noon we are duty ship, and the frigate is a dot on the horizon, heading east as fast as her engines can drive her. We barely have time to get Seddon's body to Bighi before the slip-ropes are rigged and I'm back on the wheel again, to be greeted by a force eight gale as soon as we clear the harbour. Windscoops are withdrawn and the ship is secured for heavy weather, increasing humidity in the messdecks so that a man sits in his own sweat when he takes a meal.

In true Bird Class sloop style she begins to roll her guts out at the first sniff of a swell and Tankey is immediately in trouble when he forgets to secure his spud-locker so that half a sack of murphies break loose to roll about the upper deck, bouncing and splattering underfoot. The chef passes a message round telling the cooks to send pot-mess only to the galley because he cannot keep anything more elaborate on his stove. Robby goes on walk-about with Jimmy to check for loose gear, and as always the ocean finds its way into passages to slop all over the messdecks and leave a filthy scum on the bulkheads, saturating several hammocks in the process.

To increase the discomfort we are in a hurry and have to push her along with the engines flat out, sending her smashing into coamers at a rate that has green seas bursting over the bridge. Naval ships are not designed for comfort, and the boffins tell us that a 'stiff' lively ship is a good seaboat, so we have to believe them. They don't come any sea-worthier than *Condor* for she cavorts like a gazelle with epilepsy. It looks as though it is going to be a hefty blow with the glass still plunging and force ten winds predicted. For all that, there is an air of excitement as we head eastward.

The captain is a reticent man. We all know it is an urgent mission because the peacetime Navy is not permitted to expend fuel at this rate without good reason, but he keeps us in the dark so that the buzz merchants have a field day with their wild theories. It doesn't take a genius to work out that we are chasing after an immigrant but even so some of the more imaginative members of the crew come up with some fantastic variations of their own.

There is no let-up in the weather. In fact it deteriorates until we are punching into a force ten and Robby has to call for volunteers to spend a suicidal hour securing the starboard whaler when it threatens to break loose. Under his expert guidance no one suffers more than a few bruises and they retire below, raw-handed, tired and soaked. For once, Jimmy does the right thing and they each get an extra tot for their efforts.

The boarding party is called to collect their gear on the third morning. They fall in for inspection just outside my office so I leave my door ajar so that I can eavesdrop on what goes on while Jimmy and Petty Officer Bold looks them over. Each man wears a helmet with a hard leather neck-guard, an arm-shield and a crutch piece. They are armed with long batons, lead-weighted and shaped like baseball bats, .38 revolvers, and stenguns, with pouches of ammunition strapped to their chests.

It is cumbersome equipment, not really designed to make things easy for a bloke who has to leap from one ship to another in the face of a mob who will do everything they can to make sure he falls between the two moving hulls.

'You can take off your gear for the moment,' Jimmy tells them after the inspection. 'Remain in your messes and wait to be called.'

The Monday Mutiny

One brave soul summons up enough courage to enquire, 'What are we gonna board, sir?'

'You'll find out soon enough, lad,' blares Bold. 'You may not be required at all. Just stay ready and don't go slopin' off.'

Jimmy goes by my door on his way to the bridge and the boarding-party is dismissed. I consider the blank pad of blotting-paper on my desk and wonder what great harm would be done if someone told these blokes what they are about to be asked to do. I shrug it off. One thing for sure, they would not have been called if something wasn't in the offing, so there is every chance something is visible from up top. I stow away my pens and paper and slide the door shut behind me as I make for the nearest ladder.

It's murder up here with the wind blasting my breath away and solid chunks of ocean bursting inboard to drench me every time she rolls. I have to time my dash to the ladder leading up to the Bofors gun deck carefully, and when I do make it I find several of the crew sheltering in the lee of the funnel. I look out over a foam-crested range of hills moving across the ocean in wild formation, spilling wraiths of spume in the wind. *Condor* smashes her hull through the surf, one minute lifting her stern high with white foam washing over the depth-charge racks, and the next thumping down hard when her bow rides clear of an advancing wall of solid water.

Most of the watch-on-deck are here. Some waiting their turn to take a half hour stint on the wheel, for thirty minutes is enough in this sea when *Condor* is in a bitchy mood. Determined to fall away from a head sea with no warning, so that it takes a lot of helm to bring her back before she broaches. Anticipation is the answer, reading the signs so that you can beat her at her own game, and that takes real concentration.

The only other ship in sight is a grey freighter on the same course as us. She looks like a five thousand-tonner with all her superstructure amidships. Square-bridged and

The Monday Mutiny

tall-funnelled, with samson posts set in pairs fore and aft. She rides much better than we do, taking headseas in her stride and throwing the bulk of them aside so that only the after well-deck gets wet. I feel the revolutions dropping as we slow down to keep station with her, and as I watch the Bay Class frigate comes into view ahead of her, a reflection of us with her nose buried in a big swell and water streaming from her scuppers.

So this is the cause of all the panic, and the quick dash from Malta. As if to confirm my thoughts a Catalina flying-boat swoops in low across our stern to bank and fly up the freighter's port side at mast height. She doesn't have the appearance of an illegal immigrant for her decks are clear, and there is no sign of temporary toilets and ancillary superstructure required to cope with hundreds of passengers. A signal-lamp starts to send a message from her bridge.

'Cheeky sod!'

I jerk my head round to see Sparks Wilson's beard standing straight out like a hairy wind-sock as he reads the signal.

'Says he will welcome a party of unarmed guests on board when the weather abates.'

I chuckle quietly. 'He's no fool. He knows we are outside the three-mile limit and won't want to risk an international incident. If I'm not mistaken that is a Yankee ship.'

'If she ain't flyin' an ensign, we've a right to board 'er.'

'Ah, Sparks me old son. It ain't that simple. Remember, there are a lot of people on the side of the Jews. I don't reckon the skipper will want to rub the Yanks up the wrong way. Anyway it looks like the bastard is taking the initiative; what's he saying now?'

'Nothin', 'e's just answering our lamp.'

The tannoy crackles into life, pouring static into the wind as though someone is composing his words. At last the skipper's voice lifts over the blustering wind and I get closer to the loud-speaker.

'This is the captain. The boarding party may stand down. The ship you see on our port beam is the *Pan Liberator*. We believe she is a potential illegal immigrant, so we will escort her into Famagusta where she will be placed under arrest – that's all.'

'Famagusta!' breathes Sparks with relish. 'That's a bloody good run, especially if you go inter the Turkish part of the town.'

'I thought it was out of bounds?'

'So is botin' yer rum,' he chortles wickedly as he dodges between incoming waves to go below. I follow him, but I am not so lucky and I catch a dollop, needing to hang on to one of the cutter's davits while half a ton of sea-water tries to tear me away from my hand-hold.

All that day and into the night the storm rages, but by dawn we are in the lee of Cyprus, sliding into calm water in the bay of Famagusta.

Once we are safely anchored I go out for my first look at Cyprus. There is a small harbour reaching out from beneath the town that rises like a backdrop up the hillside. To the right as I look at it the brown sprawl of the walled-in Turkish town clutters the sea-front, while further to the north a wide sweep of scrubland, open and derelict, lines the shore. When I look closer I see the huddled wooden huts and wire enclosures where the immigrants wait while their future is decided.

'Poor bastards!' I think to myself. Some have spent a lifetime waiting and now they wait again, so that each day is wasted as though a huge clock ticks away their lives, and each tick marks a lost period, never to be regained or made use of. For them it has always been tomorrow – never today. Even when they have sighted the coast of their promised land the waiting is not over, and they are herded together by foreign-speaking men to wait again.

I switch my gaze south to the town and harbour, then further south to where the broad expanse of other bays stretch into the distance with no substantial buildings to mar the skyline. Perhaps one day developers will build hotels along this attractive shore, but now only a ridge of scrub-crested sand lifts into the sky, and in one corner the RAF have built a lido with kiosks, a small jetty, and rafts floating in the limpid water with sun-tanned off-duty men and women basking like painted seals.

We send our cutter there each day with swimming parties to join in the frolics and find it is a very pleasant spot to while away a make and mend.

The strangest thing as far as I'm concerned is the way the weather behaves. Each morning we wake to a stillness that accentuates every sound and leaves the sea smooth, with an unbroken sheen like a skin on the surface. When our cutter makes its first trip ashore it spreads wide unbroken folds in convex arcs towards the beach, yet by noon the wind springs up to churn the sea into a cauldron.

I am standing at the rail watching a school of porpoise performing acrobatics when Robby comes to stand with me.

'I must be a suspicious bastard by nature,' he muses.

'Why?' I ask abstractly, watching one of the porpoise leap clear of the sea to hang for a second or two before splashing down in a welter of foam.

'Because I reckon there's somethin' goin' on over there.' He nods at the freighter. 'You watch her fo'c'sle carefully and you'll see a head pop up over the gun'l every now and again. I've bin watchin' for some time.'

I follow his gaze and stare at the dark silhouette, studying the clean sweep of her fore-peak without seeing any movement. I shake my head doubtfully. 'I don't see anything, mate. Anyway, what would it signify if I did? We only allow her enough fuel each day to keep her generators going – she can't go far.'

'What if she ain't using the fuel? What if she's burnin' other things, bits of wood and gash? Just enough to keep her lights working. What if they've accumulated enough oil to run the engines? You see, I think they are liftin' 'er 'ook by 'and, link by link.'

I look into his sober, experienced eyes then back to the freighter; shading my eyes to peer intently at the fo'c'sle. This time we both see the movement. One brief glimpse of a head bobbing up above the bulwark. A few seconds later it happens again. There is no doubt at all. Someone is working up there, and unless they are only three foot tall they're making a big effort to stay out of sight.

'We'll have to tell Jimmy,' I say urgently.

'Hah. Chance would be a fine thing!' he snorts. 'All the "pigs" are in the whaler practisin' for the regatta. As far as I know only the engineer is on board.'

'We'll have to go straight to the skipper.'

'He's away too – he's the coxswain.'

'Bloody hell!' I think hard for a second. 'It's up to us then. You go and tell the engineer what's going on. Ask him to get steam on the winch and prepare for sea. You'll have to get the cutter inboard while I signal the whaler.'

I am already climbing up to the bridge when he nods agreement, and I waylay a startled signalman. 'Hoist the church pennant with the second whaler's number quickly,' I tell him.

That's the recall and I emphasize it with a long toot on the siren, making sure they've seen it.

'D'ye hear there!' the tannoy shouts. 'Cable party muster on the fo'c'sle. Special Sea Dutymen close up. Clear lower deck. All hands man the falls to hoist the motor cutter.'

I look at the freighter. She is making no effort to hide her movements now. The bustle on our upper-deck is enough to tell her she's been rumbled and I see a wisp of steam rising from their winch. The rattle of her cable comes drifting down on the wind.

'What the dickens is going on?' Subby is standing there with his shirt-tails flapping and his hair tussled as though he has been dragged from his bunk. I should have realised he was too slightly built to make an oarsman. 'Thank God you're here, sir.' I tell him and launch into a brief explanation while he tucks his shirt into his trousers.

The Monday Mutiny

'What do you want me to do?' The shout comes from the captain of the fo'c's'le who has come aft to yell up from 'B' gun deck. I look at Subby and he leaps into the situation with enthusiasm. A glance outboard shows the whaler rowing like mad for the ship with about fifty yards to go. The skipper is standing in the stern-sheets urging them on, and if I had time to gloat I would enjoy the spectacle of Jimmy sweating at his oar.

'Weigh the anchor!' shouts Subby past my left ear. He has a wild gleam in his eyes and he is lapping the whole thing up as he goes to look over the starboard rail where Robby and a motley crowd of cooks, stewards, writers, stores assistants and every other odd bod hauling at the cutter's falls.

'You'd better go to the wheelhouse, Coxswain,' he calls over his shoulder.

It is falling into place like magic. Months of training are paying off as each man takes his place to carry on without need for orders. I spare a glance at the freighter before I disappear into the wheelhouse, in time to see the blades of her propeller begin to rotate. Her cable is up and down now, and her hook must be broken out of the ground for she is moving slowly in a wide circle to line up with the mouth of the bay.

'Too late, you sod!' I shout triumphantly, and as if in response the skipper's voice comes from the bridge:

'Half ahead together – port thirty!'

The ship shudders as she gets away from a standing start.

'Midships – meet her – steady on one three five!' I repeat the orders as our bow comes round in line with the freighter, and to complete the freighter's mortification the distant shape of our relief sloop comes up over the horizon, and she is an exact image of us except for the numbers painted on her side. I respond to another call from the bridge.

'When you are relieved I wish to see you and the Chief Bos'n's mate on the bridge,' the voicepipe says.

'Aye aye, sir.'

The captain's ascetic veneer stays firm as he compliments

us on the way we reacted to the emergency, giving the impression that he finds it all a necessary chore and is much relieved when he is able to change the subject. He sweeps his eyes over the gathering which includes Jimmy, Subby and Border.

'That ship was meant to pick up immigrants from secret rendezvous along the South European coast,' he goes on with more relish. 'However, thanks to Seddon, the Navy managed to locate and hound her so much that she was forced to change tactics and head east. We think she became part of a plan for a mass break-out from the detention camps in Cyprus, and because of your prompt action we have foiled that too. I can assure you that she will be going nowhere for some time once we have her in Haifa.'

He takes a breath before continuing. 'We will be going alongside the oiling jetty to take on fuel and supplies. Therefore it will be necessary to rig bottom lines so that we can drag the hull for limpet mines. Armed sentries will be posted on the upper deck day and night, and the cutter will carry out harbour patrols, dropping two-pound charges to deter frogmen, so no one will get much sleep, I'm afraid.

'Shore leave will be granted until twenty hundred hours and liberty-men will carry arms. Avoid no-go areas and obey instructions from the security forces implicitly. Apart from that make sure the men are alert and on their toes at all times for their own safety, and more importantly, the safety of the ship. That's all.'

We secure alongside the jetty, opposite an ex-Canadian Castle Class corvette looking dejected now she has been stripped of her warpaint. She was arrested with a cargo of immigrants some time ago and brought in by two destroyers. Now no one wants her, and she waits to find out her destiny.

The *Pan Liberator* drops anchor well out in the bay and the army swarms aboard like locusts along with a few of our lads to search her from keel to truck. They rip out panels in her cabins, drop down into her messy bilges to scratch about in remote recesses, and examine rafts, lifeboats, even her hollow samson-posts, and all the time her skipper, a surprisingly youthful fair-headed man with half a cigar perpetually planted in his mouth, smiles wryly at the antics going on in his ship.

I go across with Jimmy on one occasion in time to hear the Yank proclaim in a voice designed to carry, 'They are ripping my ship apart for no God-damned reason and Uncle Sam ain't gonna like it one little bit.'

He talks to no one in particular, but he makes sure his words reach a small group of civilians who are watching the proceedings with brooding interest. They are independent observers, part of a special commission sent to monitor the situation – no easy task from where I'm standing.

At the end of a very long day everyone is hot, sticky and bad-tempered because we have found nothing more ominous than a few signal rockets. Her crew voice loud protests to anyone who will listen at the way their ship is being treated, and at the end of it all the independent observers are no wiser. Even a cold shower does little to cheer me up, so despite the skipper's warning I suggest to Robby that we both need a run ashore.

'If I don't get off this sod for an hour or so I'll go crazy,' I tell him.

He snorts. 'Thanks for the invitation. I was gonna get me 'ousewife out and do some sewing. My number threes are fallin' apart at the seams.'

'You don't have to convince me; I've seen your working uniform and it's a bloody disgrace. When we get back to Malta and the naval tailors come on board you are going to get measured for a suit, my disreputable friend.'

He snorts again. 'I've got an allotment with Bernards. Can't remember how much I've got in the kitty.'

'Judging by the state of your gear I'd say you've amassed a small fortune. It's about time you splashed out a bit, you're giving the ship a bad name.'

'I reckon we ought to take Caruana with us. He can

speak the lingo, and he don't get ashore much.'

The chief steward is happy to come with us when we leave the ship and wander into the maze of streets and alleyways that is Haifa. It is a sobering experience with army patrols and police everywhere, taking the romance out of the local atmosphere. I find myself watching every shaded corner, and each time we look like turning into some back alley in search of local colour we find our way barred by the authorities in one shape or another.

Eventually we sit resignedly in a small cafe supping coffee while the steward carries on a quiet conversation with a couple of Palestinians. Apparently Arabic and the Maltese language have a lot in common. Robby and I watch the world go by the open doorway until suddenly one of the Arabs slaps a friendly hand on my shoulder and I look to Caruana for an explanation.

'He says we are the friends of the Arabs; the true people of Palestine, and it is good that we sit here drinking together like this. For generations their ancestors have lived in this land, so they have become part of the very sand and stone on which they walk. It belongs to them, like England belongs to you. Now these impostors come and say this is their land and that they will teach us how to make it prosper. We say to them, "What is prosperity if you have no pride?"

'These are the things that fill these men with hate, so that the very sound of a Hebrew voice twists their guts and sends fire through their veins. These strangers who come to take their land do not even speak with a common tongue. They speak German, Russian, Polish, English, and are as alien to the desert and the East as you are. No one has the right to take another man's heritage. Is that not why you fought the Germans?'

The Maltese steward spits out the words as though he feels their hate and has an axe of his own to grind. He makes no effort to hide his derision when he talks of the British and their claim to be mediators. Like many of his fellow islanders he doesn't see the average matelot as anything more than a pawn in a political game.

'You see,' he goes on as if he is still interpreting, 'Germany occupied countries with armour and bombers – the Jews invade under the guise of friendship, using money to wrest the land from under the feet of the natives, and in many cases the chequebook is more persuasive than the sword.'

I'm getting sick to the back teeth with all this talk. It seems you can't get away from politics anywhere, and now I am beginning to regret coming on this run ashore.

'Joe!' I call, and the proprietor lifts his head to grin at me. 'Let's have a round of beer.' He reaches under the counter and I see his eyes widen as a black object hurtles through the open doorway.

I have only a split second to recognise its pineapple shape and the open lever before I dive for the floor yelling, 'Grenade!'

The room splits apart and there is a rushing sound in my ears like an express train. The air fills with dust and I swim in a grey blur as I feel my body lifted into a whirlpool of tangled arms and legs. Gradually the blur resolves into dark, solid shapes when I struggle onto my elbows. A dead weight slumps on me, and warm, sticky moisture is oozing into my clothing.

The shapes take form and I can see colours. Brown legs and khaki shorts coming towards me from out of the haze.

'Where does it hurt, Jack?' an anxious voice asks.

'Where doesn't it hurt!' I'm thinking as I try to find the source of real agony. Strangely enough I seem to be in one piece, and my hearing is improving. There's blood pouring from a leg wound and my head and arms are full of cuts and scrapes, but instinctively I know that I am not seriously injured.

'It's okay, mate,' I reassure the kneeling pongo, cautiously easing myself upright and gazing about. The dust still hangs in the air and there is smoke pouring from a small fire in one corner. I lurch towards the daylight, forcing my body through a ring of rubbernecks as they crane in to savour the slaughter. Even the rancid smell of the street is like a tonic when I draw breath. My brain begins to function, and as I regain my senses I get another thought.

'Robby!' I shout, forcing my way back in again. I find him sitting on a pile of rubble with two medical orderlies holding him upright. There is blood all over his face but his eyes are open, although he stares vaguely into space, muttering incoherently.

'Robby,' I bend to get close and his eyes swivel agitatedly, searching for my voice. He's in a hell of a state and I place a hand on him. 'You'll be okay now, mate. You're scratched about a bit but Monday will soon sort you out. Just take it easy now.'

His bleeding lips twist into a half-smile. 'Okay, Ben. I'll be glad when some bastard gets the lights working though.'

I look at the orderly. Brilliant sunshine floods in through the open doorway and I read the truth in his eyes. 'Leave it to us, Jack,' he says kindly as Robby's eyes swim about, trying to pierce the darkness that surrounds him. I back off and allow them to place him gently on a stretcher. They cover his eyes with bandage, but I still see the empty stare as he looked directly into the light, and I begin to weep.

I ignore the stares as I go out until someone tugs at my sleeve.

'This yours?' A sergeant hands me a rifle and I accept it dumbly. I wouldn't know if it was but Bold will want to check it off on his list when I get back to the ship. Reaction is setting in now and I'm feeling sick.

'Jump into the jeep. We'll take you back to your ship.' A hand supports me as I reel in the centre of a ring of faces. The dust is settling now, and I can see into the café where they are dragging out bodies.

One of the orderlies comes to me. 'Your other mate. I – I'm afraid he's a gonner.' The voice is sympathetic but matter-of-fact, as though he's seen it all before and has tried not to become immune. I allow him to guide me to the jeep. Every jolt sends a spasm through me as we drive through the narrow streets, choked with a chaos of vehicles, people and donkeys. Someone holds on to my waistband to stop me rolling out when I vomit over the side.

The news has reached the ship ahead of us for Monday and Jimmy are waiting when we reach the ship. 'Nancy' is quartermaster, looking out of place in his webbing with a .38 revolver hanging from his belt. I shake off the helping hands before crossing the plank and pull myself upright to regain a little dignity. It is difficult though, for congealed blood is setting hard on my filthy face and I am capless and ragged. Monday takes my arm to lead me below to his sickbay. Once inside he ignores my protests and settles me into one of the cots. Louvres pump air into the sickbay and all sound is muffled outside the closed door while he dabs at my wounds, carefully cleaning away the muck. I hardly notice the doctor when he comes to check me over before jabbing a needle into my arm.

Much later when I wake I sense the vibration of the screws. Monday has his back to me as he fiddles with something on his desk. 'We at sea?' I croak through swollen lips.

'Shifting berth,' he replies without looking up. 'We are going to anchor out in the bay. Try to lie still until the doc comes to look at you.'

'I'm dying for a piss.'

'Use this,' he offers a bottle, and while I fill it he sticks a thermometer under my tongue. That shuts me up while he removes the bottle and takes my pulse.

'Any chance of some grub?'

'Not until the quack's been to see you,' he grins. 'That's a good sign – means you're getting better.'

'Don't kid yourself. I'm not hungry. I just think I'll recover quicker if I eat something.'

'What bloody rubbish! You've had a traumatic

experience. You don't get over it that easily.'

I struggle up onto my pillows. 'My lack of appetite has nothing to do with my physical condition. You know about Robby?'

'Yes.'

'The bastards!'

He comes across with a bowl of hot water. 'Here, have a wash.'

I hold it in my lap for a moment looking at him. 'What do you think of your Jewish friends now?'

'They're not my friends, Swain, any more than they are my enemies. Stay quiet until the doc comes.' He rinses out a facecloth. 'Here, perhaps it would be easier if I do it.'

'Piss off!' I snatch it away violently, spilling water on the bed. 'I'll do it myself.' While I wash I watch him closely. 'You can't sit on the fence, Monday. Go soft and they will walk right over us; that's the nature of things. They have blinded Robby and killed Caruana and Seddon. What more will it take to convince you?'

'Try not to get excited, Swain.'

'For Christ's sake!' I holler at him, tipping the bowl and contents over everything and swinging my legs out of the cot to face him, filled with a blinding rage. 'I've just seen my best mate blinded, you pillock! And you've got the gall to tell me not to get excited! People like you make me sick!'

'Get back into your bed, Swain,' he says calmly, and grabs my arm with a grip that surprises me. Whatever the doctor pumped into me last night weakens me so that I cannot resist him when he pushes me back into the cot. 'Let's face it, Swain. You don't know who threw the grenade. In fact, like the rest of us you haven't a clue what it is all about. You can't believe those poor bastards on the immigrant ships have anything to do with these terrorists surely?'

'You can't separate them, Monday. In a conflict like this everyone has to be on one side or the other – like it or not. Or are you too bloody stupid to see that?'

'I would have thought you had grown out of that by now,' he says thoughtfully.

'Grown out of what?'

'The business of training blokes until they are like machines, itching to have a go, then sending them in to duff-up some poor bastard without really knowing what it is all about. You know, Chief, before I left the UK I saw a train-load of matelots on their way to Liverpool to join a troopship. There were inflated french-letters hanging from the windows and some of the stupid young idiots had chalked "Look out, Haifa; here we come" on the carriage doors – poor mindless sods.'

That does it. The hurt and anger wells up and I hurl myself at him.

'*Stop that at once!*'

The army doctor is standing in the doorway. 'What in hell's name is going on?' He closes the door and looks from one to the other. Monday is pulling himself together in one corner. There is a bruise on his face and a trickle of blood running down one cheek where I must have hit him.

'Delirious, sir. He woke a minute ago and went berserk.' He dabs cautiously at his forehead. 'I think he's okay now.'

The doctor is unconvinced but decides to let things ride. 'Get back into bed. I'll see if you're fit for duty.'

By mid-afternoon I am on the wheel again as we leave the anchorage in response to an urgent signal from a Norwegian tanker who is standing by a ship packed with immigrants who have survived the gales we went through and now she lies dead in the water, disabled and in distress, with many of her people in a very bad way. The Norwegian captain offered to take off the sick, or indeed everyone if they wished to abandon but they refused, telling him they intend to remain together for they are only ten miles from the Palestinian coast.

We should reach her in less than three hours and that will leave enough daylight to board her and get the engine going, or if necessary take her in tow. There is time to have a meal before the boarding-party draw their gear from the GI's store, and the remainder of the ship's company go to their stations.

I go to stand on the quarterdeck as we swing out of the bay, looking back at the receding shore with its cluster of huddled houses and moored ships, and I see a pall of black smoke rising like a pillar into the pale blue sky. I half expect a familiar voice to offer some comment, and think of Robby's weathered features with its sober expression and feel choked. The thought of him never being able to inspect a 'turkshead' or a well-stowed whaler is unbearable.

I go below to my office and my tot, sickened with the sadness inside me and feeling the hot surge of hate building up. War had one advantage. The enemy wore a coal-scuttle helmet and was as faceless as a bloody punchbag, and if you didn't kill him, he killed you. The trouble with this lot is that they have faces that stare back at you with reproachful eyes, and you can't push away the fact that you are dealing with people.

'Bah!' I grunt aloud and take another sip. I'm thinking again, and thinking is for the likes of Monday who is so busy trying to work things out he becomes bloody useless in an emergency so that you can't rely on him when it matters. After this trip I am going to have to do something about him.

Five

Condor works up to full speed within an hour as we steam south towards the immigrant ship and her Norwegian escort. The long coastline of Palestine is with us for most of the way, but fades behind a heat haze when we are in sight of the big tanker. As always the Scandinavian ship puts many of our own merchant ships to shame with her immaculate appearance, and her signal-lamp is already blinking at us as we close on her. As I watch through the port wheelhouse door she moves sedately in a wide arc and settles on a westerly course, dipping her ensign as she goes. She is a busy lady, and much relieved to be on her way once more. As she picks up speed, she opens up a view of the immigrant and we get our first real look at her.

It is a sight to melt the heart of the most hard-nosed seaman. I recognise the *Empire Seasilver* at once, even though her silhouette is changed by an assortment of additional deck-houses, including open latrines built out over her sides which have suffered damage in the gales. There are extra life-rafts too, lashed to every available space, and the lifeboats are doubled up one above the other at the davits in a fashion that would turn a government inspector's hair grey. I shudder to think what chaos would ensue if they tried to lower those boats in a hurry. She is listing over to port, so that her deck is open to us as we creep in slowly, allowing time for the captain to study her.

When I glance fore and aft I notice many of our off-duty men on deck, and every face seems to wear the same pitying expression when they see the pathetic cargo she carries. The immigrants are just anonymous shapes from this distance. Mostly black and grey, with pale oval faces peering out at us. Even in the warm sunshine they look cold, and I sense their resentment even from here.

The sloop closes in stealthily as though we are stalking a quarry, and as we come round to the immigrant's sunny side I can read her new name, *Star of Judea*, painted in large white letters on her hull. 'Some bloody star!' I think to myself as I watch her rolling like a waterlogged chunk of drift-wood in the long swell. Now her stink drifts down to us on the light breeze and it churns my guts. God knows what sort of mess she is in below decks where the Jews are battened down in their airless dungeon, swimming with hog-wash and vomit. At that moment I make up my mind to break with tradition and even as the pipe shrills to call us to boarding stations I am climbing to the bridge.

Jimmy sees me coming and demands angrily, 'What is it, Coxswain?'

I chop him off a brief salute. 'I'd like to go with the boarding-party, sir. I think Monday should go too – there will be sick people on board that ship.'

'Allow us some credit,' he sneers. 'Don't you think we have thought of that? Monday is going, but your place is on the wheel and you cannot be spared.'

'Why do you want to go, Coxswain?' The captain is peering over Jimmy's shoulder at me.

'I know her master, sir. I met him in Weymouth. It might help if he sees a familiar face. Anyway, I think she will need a tow, and we'll need extra hands over there. I know the layout of her cabins and Leading Seaman Richardson is more than capable of handling the helm here.' It all sounds pretty lame, and I am not even sure of my own motives.

The wind comes breathing over the fore-part of the bridge, singing through the metalwork while they study my face. I know Jimmy is suspicious; he knows full well the relationship between Robby and me and must be worried that I might be nursing a heavy grudge against the Jews, but the skipper seems to recognise something in my expression that convinces him I am on the level.

'All right, Grant, you can go. I agree you could probably be more use over there, but you will stay back until the last section of the boarding-party goes, then make your way straight to the wheelhouse, do you understand? The men will have enough on their hands without spare NCOs confusing the issue. Draw webbing and a revolver, and report back up here again in five minutes.' He turns to Jimmy. 'I want to see Sub-Lieutenant Connaught, Stoker Petty Officer Marsh and Petty Officer Bold before we go in.'

He gives us a pep talk and explains why I am going with them. For once he drops his mask of remote arrogance and there is concern in his eyes. It is at moments like this when I realise the awesome responsibility that weighs on a captain's shoulders, and it never ceases to amaze me that the hierarchy seem to get it right more often than not when they appoint these men. There will always be bad skippers, but they are rare and don't tend to stay long in command. Some who begin badly take on a new mantle after initiation as they gain confidence and earn the respect of their crews.

Today our captain has a special responsibility, for recently lives were lost on a boarding that went sadly wrong. We are being watched by many nations, and the decisions of men like our skipper come under scrutiny when they order their men to board these immigrant ships. Now he gives a great deal of thought before issuing his first orders. He searches our faces as he speaks, making sure his words are understood.

'Hopefully there will be no need to use strongarm tactics this time. By the look of her she is in desperate need of assistance and will accept our help, albeit reluctantly. With any luck she will allow us to come on board without hindrance, and I intend to request that we do so without waiting until we are inside the three-mile limit so that we can take her in tow if her engine cannot be started.

The Monday Mutiny

'Once you are on board get to your stations as quickly and unobtrusively as possible. It is up to you to assess the situation and signal a report to me immediately, Sub. No heroics please. If we are invited to go on board we must behave ourselves impeccably. There may be a few hot-heads amongst them and I rely on you to quell any resistance with minimum force. Difficult I know, but that is why you received special training.'

He relaxes a little. 'I have decided to send the coxswain and Leading Sickberth Attendant Monday with you because you will find sick, possibly even injured amongst the immigrants. The more we can turn this into a mission of mercy the better. We may even establish a liaison with the Jews, and if we could achieve that it would be a triumph indeed. If necessary I will send Lieutenant Border too, but only if you request it, Sub. There is no reason why you should feel isolated if you follow the drill. We will never be far away, although obviously I cannot keep the ship alongside in this swell. It remains only to wish you good luck. Keep calm, don't over-react, and maybe we will do this thing without any real aggression.'

There is an uncanny silence emanating from the sad little ship and her cargo of misery. The skipper hails her through a loud-speaker. His plummy voice distorted so that it seems to fill the air with echoing sound. We hold off about twenty yards abeam of her low side and we can see that most of those on deck have climbed to her starboard side in an effort to counterbalance the list. Even up-wind the stench of her primitive latrines is obvious and I can see the filth staining her sides beneath the open pans.

There must be many more immigrants below in her hold and I find it hard to imagine the nightmarish conditions that prevail down there in the dim light. Shifting my gaze to her wheelhouse I see several figures standing in a group watching us with cold, hostile eyes; in contrast to the desperate resentment registered on the faces of the mass in her waist.

There he is! The same square-jawed, fair-headed man I met outside Seddon's cabin. Standing tall amongst the others with the sleeves of his open-necked shirt rolled up over his brawny arms. A hot anger consumes me as I look at him, for I remember how I mistook him for a seaman with seaman's values. Now I am looking at a cold-blooded villain who could be one of those old-time slavers, calculating their profit by the numbers they could cram head to tail in the stinking holds of the ships they commanded. This is the bastard who probably murdered Seddon, or at least conspired to have him killed. I glare at him, hoping my stare will drill into him so that he will look in my direction and see my disgust, but he is staring at our bridge with no real expression in his face.

'Do you require assistance?' The skipper's voice booms out across the water.

We have no right to board her by force until she enters the three mile limit and the way she is drifting that could take forever, depending on the current. With luck they will see sense and realise how much they need our help. Surely even that self-centred sod of a skipper will have some concern for his passengers.

No such luck with this bastard though. He doesn't even bother to answer as an assortment of missiles is hurled at us from the midst of the crowd. Canned food, spuds, even eggs drop short, but the message is patently clear. All he does is wave a contemptuous arm and disappear inside his wheelhouse.

I turn to Subby. 'Now what, sir?'

'If the captain decides there is danger to life he might over-ride her master and take things into his own hands. He might assume it his duty to board her by force if necessary.'

The metallic voice fills the air between the two ships once more. 'I have been called to your assistance and I consider you to be in imminent danger of foundering. Therefore I am coming alongside to put some men on board.'

A strong jet of steaming water arcs out from her,

The Monday Mutiny

accompanied by a low growl of protest and a forest of waving fists. Many of the men are holding improvised weapons, and prominent among them is a burly individual wearing a white apron and brandishing a meat-cleaver.

We have a net awning rigged over the fo'c'sle to protect our boarding party while they make their preparations as we close in. The captain takes *Condor* in a wide circle to make his approach from her port quarter to come up on her low side. Petty Officer Bold and Subby move amongst their men checking that they are correctly equipped, and know exactly what is expected of them. I stand well back behind Marsh's small group which includes Sparks Wilson and a senior signalman. The *Star of Judea* is rolling more than ever now as she lies broadside to the swell, and we lower big fenders over the side as the two ships come together.

Our men are poised ready. Watching the heaving, sloping deck as the last few yards are eaten up and trying to ignore the barrage of cat-calls and missiles being thrown at them. It is a delicate manoeuvre, with the low side of the small ship only a couple of feet or so above sea-level. One false move could bring disaster, for if we punch a hole in her side she will flood instantly. Today, however, the weather is kind to us as the skipper brings our starboard bow up to the tiny poop-deck, for this is where it will be easiest to board. It is the least crowded part of the ship and each upward roll brings it within reach of our rail. The trick is to wait for both vessels to combine their roll so that the two decks come level. The first men grip their long batons tightly, watching the narrowing gap and the threatening immigrants waiting for them. Knowing that when they jump they will be on their own, if their mates don't follow at once before the ships roll apart. The one thing in our favour is that she is without power, otherwise she would be dodging and wriggling like a demented eel.

'*Go go go!*'

Petty Officer Bold's yell pierces the atmosphere above the chaos as he jumps straight into the face of a waiting man. There is no doubting the PO's courage as he launches himself into the mob. Tearing into them like a tornado, shouting encouragement to his men all the time. A one-man assault; forcing his way with no thought for his own safety. A cheer goes up from the waiting seamen and a blue avalanche of boarders pours after him, beating about them with the same wild fury, to drive a wedge through the mass until the poopdeck is clear of opposition.

The two ships hang together and I go with my section, feeling the same thrill of excitement welling inside as I become incensed. I find myself yelling with them and scrambling on the sloping deck towards the wheelhouse. A surge of triumph runs through me when I close the door and glance out to see our sailors ranging themselves in a disciplined line across the front of the bridge. Bold is drilling them as though they are on a parade-ground.

It was all too easy. When I get my breath back and look about the answer is simple. Apart from the few hot-heads who were responsible for the barrage of missiles and resistance to Bold's over-enthusiastic assault, the immigrants have accepted the boarding with resignation. Now they are crowded together in the waist, staring up at us with a kind of sad resentment written on their faces.

Despite her appearance she is a fairly new ship, but built in austere times when the only requirement was that she should be capable of running wartime supplies and landing parties between Pacific islands and be able to beach on remote bays. Everything is utility despite the efforts of her present owner to introduce furnishings to make her more acceptable to peacetime crews. The fittings in the wheelhouse must have been changed for they are British, and the standard magnetic compass is set in a brass binnacle behind a man-sized wheel that dominates the area. When I try the spokes steering chains rattle through the runners and guides to the yoke of the tiller. It is a primitive arrangement with no mechanical aid to help the

The Monday Mutiny

helmsman. I guess that in a heavy sea it would be a two-handed job to keep her on course. Especially when she is overloaded like now.

There is an open bridge above the wheelhouse and I hear the boots of several seamen clumping about up there. Things are quieting down now that we are established, as though the Jews are exhausted after their initial show of aggression. Strain is showing in the faces of all except a few of the hard cases, and although their faces are hostile they are too exhausted to resist any more.

There is a bustle of activity near the door and an ERA hurries through to drop down into the engineroom hatch. *Condor* is circling slowly, looking smart with her Mediterranean grey paint gleaming in the sunshine. There is a pink tinge to the light now, and when I look to starboard the sky is stained with the first flush of sunset, spreading a twinking path across the sea towards us from the big orange orb of the sinking sun.

Apart from the slop of the bilges there are other sounds. The murmur of voices and the general bustle of human beings settling themselves into any corner where they can brace their bodies against the list and roll. Until now her skipper has stood with his back against the after bulkhead watching us with narrow, defiant eyes as we take over his ship, and Subby has seen fit to ignore his presence while the men are organised into their different stations. When I turn to look our eyes meet and a brief flash of recognition crosses his face. I make no effort to conceal my contempt for him, but he shows no reaction at all.

A hefty cough followed by a growing rhythmic beat of a diesel comes from below and a dirty lightbulb hanging from a frayed wire glows dimly and livens into a pale glow. The sky is streaked brilliant with ribbons of scarlet and gold, and the edges of clouds grow rich with colour. The whole ship is bathed in the warm glow and groups of immigrants turn violet and mauve as they merge into shadowy corners.

The Monday Mutiny

A kind of melancholia takes over as though the first breath of night invades our souls and leaves us shamed by what we are about.

The long, rolling coastline has come into view, reflecting the sunset with a sullen hue, lifeless and dismal in the afterglow. Torpedo-men are rigging wandering leads to add more light when darkness arrives and the ERA reports the generator working, although the main engine is beyond repair. Our signalman uses his battery-powered aldis lamp to pass the information across to *Condor*, and while we wait for an answer I ask Subby, 'Shouldn't we put some of the leaders somewhere secure, sir? God knows what they will get up to once darkness falls.'

'Where do you suggest?'

'The cabins all lead off from a central passage. If we check them thoroughly in case there are flood-valves or weapons, and ensure the prisoners have no matches or combustibles with them, a couple of armed sentries could easily look after them. After that I suggest someone tells the rest that we intend towing the ship to safety.'

He thinks for a moment. 'I'll go along with placing the leaders under guard. Especially that fellow there.' He points at a small, wiry individual with mocking eyes and long black hair thatching a youthful face. 'I have noticed him dodging about everywhere urging on the vociferous ones. I feel sure there must be Hagana amongst this lot, organising things. That chap with the meat-cleaver for instance: he seems to have disappeared and I don't believe he is only the ship's cook. We will need to watch them carefully and put any would-be saboteurs where they can do no harm. When it comes to making speeches, however, I think that is best left until we learn what the captain plans to do about the tow.'

When I give Petty Officer Bold his orders I notice that his face is lit up as though he is intoxicated by all the excitement, and I have to repeat the orders to make certain he has taken them in. He seems to be in his element, relishing every minute as he snaps curt commands to his men.

'We'll take that one too,' he says, pointing at a youngster wearing a bright check shirt and cord trousers who is glaring at us from beneath the ladder leading up to the starboard side of the poop. Bold goes after him personally, inviting the youth to have a go, and for a moment I fear there will be a confrontation of the sort the skipper was so anxious about, but the PO jabs the muzzle of his revolver hard against the lad's cheek with the black barrel just under his left eye and that is enough to convince him. There is no fear in his eyes, just open defiance as Bold hauls him out of his corner and rams the revolver into the middle of his back.

'Get below with the rest of your scum!' the PO spits. 'One wrong move and I'll blow your guts out.'

I cringe and suck in my breath as I see Bold gloating over his captive. Whatever it is that is going rotten inside the PO I hope to God it stays dormant until this is over.

Condor's lamp is flashing, magnified right out of proportion in the gloom as the sun finally takes a dive and the brief Mediterranean twilight is snuffed out. It is a long signal, and one of the seamen takes it down as the man on the lamp dictates. The sloop intends coming alongside with extra men and towing gear. We are to secure our end of the tow to the anchor-cable then pay out half a shackle to give some spring to the hawser. To help us *Condor* has rigged lights on her starboard side to illuminate the fo'c'sle while we work.

While she makes her wide turn to come up to us Monday arrives with a small, worried-looking grey-haired man, wearing pebble-lensed glasses and a battered trilby.

'This gentleman is a doctor, sir,' introduces the SBA. 'I have been helping him down below. There are many people requiring medical attention, including a very pregnant woman. Conditions are appalling in the hold and some are in desperate need of hospital treatment.'

The Monday Mutiny

'You've been down there amongst the immigrants without my orders?' demands Subby.

'Yes, sir. I assume that is why I have been brought along.' His tone is insolent and I groan inwardly as I sense him leading up to one of his bloody crusades.

'You should have waited for orders, Monday,' I growl, trying to take the weight off Subby's shoulders.

'You were too busy knocking seven bells out of everyone,' he snaps into my face.

'That will do!' barks Subby. 'You had no right to take matters into your own hands like that. You could have been taken hostage or even killed. How the hell am I supposed to organise things if people like you go wandering off on their own?'

'Pardon, sir.' The doctor's calm voice breaks in. 'This man is wearing a red cross on his sleeve and we have great respect for the Red Cross. That is why he was allowed to come amongst us. It is good that he has seen what it is like down there.' His bearing is dignified, and he talks to Subby as though he is talking to a young man who needs to be guided through a situation he is too immature to comprehend.

'You are Doctor –?' asks Subby blandly.

The old man lifts his sleeve to reveal a number tattooed on his pale skin. 'Until I become a person again in Israel this is my identity. You must understand this is a matter of life and death.'

'We have to do something immediately!' urges Monday.

'Be quiet!' I snap. 'One more outburst like that and you'll be for the high jump!' I ease off a little. 'Now that you have broken most of the rules in the book you might just as well try to give us a proper report. Try and do it quickly and succinctly without any dramatics, we're in a hurry to get the tow rigged.' I nod in the direction of *Condor*. She seems to be taking her time most likely because she has to assemble the right men and equipment before she gets here.

Monday chokes back his frustration and spells it out to us. Every now and again the doctor intervenes, until eventually he takes over to build a graphic picture of the misery and suffering in the hold. They have come through the horror of the storm without any deaths, but some became so weak and ill they have not strength to recover.

For two days the strong have tried to clean up the mess, rigging canvas wind-scoops to feed fresh air down into the malodorous cavern where wooden bunks are tiered from deck to hatch-cover and the sick became so overcome by the violence of the weather they just vomited where they lay, soiling their own beds and those of others sleeping beneath them.

The ship threw herself about so much they could not keep their feet, and when the engine broke down the situation became a nightmare. The doctor had to fight his own sea-sickness when, for the safety of the ship, hatches had to be shut, cutting off light and air, so he worked in semi-darkness filled with the sound and smell of retching people who prayed for death to come and relieve them of their suffering while children wailed for succour. Water was rationed – allowed only for drinking and cleaning wounds, so they tried to use sea-water to wash away the filth when they could summon enough energy to attempt the impossible task.

When the storm abated there was no one left to cope. No part of the deck that was unoccupied by a slumped body with no will to move, and content to lie in the filth while the endless hours dragged by. When the crew opened the hatches they reeled back from the stench that rose out of the hold and marvelled that anyone could exist in such a noisome place; yet when they went down they found some immigrants already rising from their bunks and making vain efforts to restore order.

For two days they worked like slaves stripping bedding and tossing it overboard. Better to lie on bare boards than try to salvage the unspeakable putrescence they had slept

The Monday Mutiny

in. They searched through their paltry possessions to find clothing to replace the defiled rags that clung to the bodies of those worst affected, and gradually the squalor was scrubbed away and the sun dried the deck as the sea mellowed. At last they were able to come up top in small groups to savour the pure, fresh breeze. They ate their first meal for days and combed the knots out of their hair, then looked about them at the quiet ocean. A finger pointed and others looked to see a long coastline lifting out of the eastern horizon, and when someone dared to ask if it was Palestine the master told them 'yes'. Some went wild with joy; climbed the mast to point towards the brown hummocks, bringing forth cheers from below – others just wept.

The euphoria lasted for some time while the engineer worked to get his engine stripped to find out why it had stopped, and many of the people began to get their gear together, convinced that they were nearly home. Even when the captain stood before them and told them they could not repair the engine they would not believe their ordeal was not over, and that somehow they would drift towards the promised land.

The hours went by while they waited. The sun lost its benevolence and turned the ship into an oven where those too ill to move baked in their beds. Children became fractious or scampered about the upper deck, getting in everybody's way and increasing the growing bad temper while the ship wallowed helplessly and the coast kept its distance. When they looked for someone to vent their frustrations upon the men who failed to restart the engine became an easy target, because a new fear was growing as many realised that while they wallowed like this the British could find them.

Oblivious of all this those who had not recovered from the storm were still suffering the sickening effects of the rolling, lifeless ship: urging on empty stomachs and vomiting blood. The doctor and his small band of helpers were doing what they could with inadequate supplies of medicine and found their task impossible. Even food was rationed now, for much of their supplies had been ruined by the storm.

We have time to absorb this graphic account for *Condor* is taking a long time to make her approach. The old doctor has to take frequent rests and Monday interposes with lurid descriptions of what he has seen. Between them they paint a grim picture and I look impatiently towards the sloop as she circles well astern with dark shapes working on her quarterdeck in the glow of emergency lighting.

I know what a difficult task they have on, for they have to break out the huge hurricane-hawser from its stowage in the after four-inch gun sponson and manhandle it aft to the depth-charge platform where it must be flaked down between the rails. The sloop is not designed for towing, so the thick wire with its double bite of manilla spliced into the middle to add weight will take a lot of space.

A suitable anchorage for the tow will need to be found so that it can be guided through the after fair-leads. Jimmy will be there with the pick of his seamen POs and leading hands, working in the shadows with the heavy gear, most of which has been stowed away since the ship was commissioned. They will not wish to hurry things, for a tow that breaks free and goes wild becomes a violent reptile that can take off a man's leg. We can do no more until they are ready to come alongside, so Subby encourages the doctor to talk.

'What happened when the tanker found you?'

The old man looks puzzled for a moment. 'At first we thought she was a warship, because she was painted grey, you see. Then, as she came nearer, someone said she was a Norwegian merchant ship and we did not know what to think. By then our little ship was lying on her side because, as the captain explained, the ballast had shifted in the gale. The tanker looked immense as she came up to us. Her superstructure towered like huge cliffs and we could see faces peering down at us.

'Our captain called in English to her, and after a short time someone answered. We watched and waited, praying for I don't know what while the shouting went on. At last our captain turned to us and explained that the Norwegian captain could not become involved with an illegal ship like ours, but if there were any seriously ill or injured on board he would send a boat for them, then stand by us until it was certain we were in no danger of sinking. In the meantime his duty was to call for assistance. Deep down we all knew what this would mean, but by that time many of the older people were too tired or sick to care any more. They knew that if the British took us into their camps at least it would be in Palestine.

'Some of the young men told us that many immigrants were being taken back to Europe, but I don't think anyone really believed that.' He looks at Subby's young, serious face and his old eyes wrinkle with concern. 'You are only a boy but you must have a mother and father. Look at these people who have suffered so much and then tell me that they do not deserve a land where they can live in peace.'

He grows silent, leaving a void to be filled with the soft sounds of wind and sea while we try not to look at his embarrassed face.

'It is not for us to make these decisions, doctor; you must know that,' pleads Subby with a catch to his voice. 'One thing I can say is that the worst is over for your people.'

'Is it?' demands the old man with sudden anger. 'Do you not realise that what you see here is nothing to the suffering we feel inside? If you keep us away from our destiny now you will be damned in the eyes of the world – we will see to that.' He shuffles away, bent over with tiredness and rage.

Monday moves to face Subby, looking intently into his eyes. 'Where will this ship be towed, sir?'

'That's none of your damned business!' snaps Subby. 'Just get on with your work and leave the thinking to others. You have stuck your nose in far enough already.'

The SBA's face works as he bottles his outrage. 'Aye aye,

sir,' he replies curtly before following the old man down below. No one makes any attempt to stop him.

It looks as though *Condor* is ready at last for her signal-lamp is flashing away again, spelling out a long series of instructions for taking up the tow. It is too dark and treacherous for her to come alongside in the swell so she intends sending the cutter across with the extra hands and some bag-meals for the boarding party. The hurricane hawser is too much for the small boat so a grass-rope will be floated down to us from the sloop with a few barricos hitched on for extra buoyancy.

I wait until the cutter leaves the sloop before making my way down into the waist with a couple of ratings on our way to help the men on the fo'c'sle. This is the closest I have been to the immigrants, and as we move through the crowd I sense their hostility. Some of the younger ones watch us with narrow-eyed menace as we begin to manhandle the gear. I can feel their eyes boring into my spine as the stoker PO feeds steam to the winch, and I hear the first clank of the dogs as he tests it. We heave in the grass-rope, feeling very isolated as we work with the immigrants between us and the main party, and I'm pleased to see Petty Officer Bold coming aft to stand with two of his seamen facing aft into the mob with their weapons cocked ready to protect us.

The atmosphere is charged with tension and I know that one careless move on our part, or some wild shout from a fire-eater will stir up trouble. I get on with the job, trying not to think about them as we bring in the grass-rope.

A full moon hangs like a big medallion in the starlit sky, spreading a glittering path of silver across the ocean. It is a bitterly cold night; in dramatic contrast to the heat of the day, and the metal superstructure is icy to my touch while the cold bites through our thin clothing.

I cross my arms above my head to show that we are ready; then it is a case of standing well back as *Condor* takes up the slack. The long wire slithers up out of the sea like a serpent until it is bar-taut between the ships.

One sharp jerk could wreck all our efforts, and even cause injury now, so the sloop pulls ahead at dead slow revolutions with the long bight lifting until we feel the slight judder as the strain comes on. The links clash against the metal jaw of the fairlead and the slip springs up from the metal 'scotsman', rigid while the hawser sings with tension.

We hold our breath as *Condor* struggles to overcome the inertia, willing her to haul our bows around, and as if in response to our prayers the tow suddenly sags. Slowly, with great reluctance, the ship is swinging broadside on to the sea so that the low side of the well-deck scoops water inboard across the hatch-covers. Those on deck scramble up to the high side in a vain effort to correct the list and the two hatches allow a deluge to pour down into the hold.

Now she lifts again to swoop us up in a crazy orbital spiral until she is balanced on the crest of a long ridge of black ocean; poised for a moment before she pivots and plunges down into the trough; this time though it is a more controlled descent and her deck stays dry. Someone on the helm is helping her to line up with *Condor* and the motio is becoming less vicious all the time as we get steerage-way.

The tow is a long, dipping arc now, losing itself in the body of the sea a few yards ahead. She is following *Condor* like a docile puppy, content to be led by the sloop, so that we can relax a little.

'Watch the tow,' I tell Bold. 'I'm going aft to report to Subby. Yell if you have any problems.'

He nods without taking his eyes away from the mob. The list doesn't seem so bad now that we are heading into the sea. I can make my way aft with no need to move from handhold to handhold as before. Bodies of black oily swell move past the hull in a mysterious procession that seems to caress the ship and ease her forward. There is a low murmur of sound coming from below as I pass an open hatch, but even that sound is less aggressive now. In the dimly lit wheelhouse one of *Condor*'s seamen is on the helm. His job is simple enough, for all he has to do is keep the bow

The Monday Mutiny

lined up with the sloop's sternlight. Subby stands behind him, watching over his shoulder.

'Everything all right forward, Coxswain?' he asks when I enter.

'Fine, sir. The tow's taken up and unless there is a sudden blow we should be okay. How long do you think we'll have to keep it up?'

He ponders for a moment. 'It took about two hours to get here at full speed so I estimate about forty miles to get back to Haifa; say, about thirteen hours at three knots, which is as much as we can hope for with this list. With luck we should be rid of her by mid-morning. I must say I won't be sorry.'

'The cutter brought some food over, sir. I wonder if there's any chance of a brew. I know where the galley is.'

'A fine idea, Coxswain, but I think we ought to ask her captain. Things are moving smoothly now; let's not do anything to spoil things.'

'I would choke if I had to ask favours from that bastard, sir. Can I send someone else?'

'No, you can't pass the buck, whatever you might think of him. After all this is his ship.'

Down below the two sentries are lounging in the small passage, deep in conversation. 'Which cabin is the captain's?' I ask.

A gruff voice invites me in when I knock and I find him lying on his bunk watching me as I slide open the door.

'We've got the tow rigged, sir. We are making about three knots. With luck we should reach Haifa tomorrow morning. Would you mind if we used your galley to make a hot drink?'

He studies my face for a moment. 'I'm surprised you bothered to ask. The ship is yours, isn't it? Why get polite all of a sudden?'

Much as I try I cannot really hate this bloke. In my book he is every kind of a rat for trading in human misery like this, yet there is something about him that earns my

The Monday Mutiny

respect. He has the look of a man who takes life by the scruff of the neck and makes it work for him. I doubt if he's ever taken an order that didn't suit him, and there is no humiliation or guilt in his attitude even now. He is a square, capable man with grey, honest eyes that stare right back at you, and it doesn't suit what I know him to be: a ruthless sod without scruples.

'I'm just an NCO, sir. It's up to the officer, but maybe if you gave him your word he would allow you on the bridge.'

'Only an NCO!' he laughs, staring into my face. 'You're the one who came on board in Weymouth. I think you're more than an NCO. I think you've got opinions, sailor; and I would like to know what's on your mind.'

I stare back at him, weighing my words carefully. 'I've tried to reason out the situation, and the more I ponder over it the more complicated it gets. One thing I'm certain of; some people are making money out of all this and they don't give a toss about the rights and wrongs of it. In my book, sir, they are leeches, and they are sucking the blood of others who are in a situation over which they have no control.'

To my astonishment he is grinning widely. 'You've got it all worked out, haven't you?' He swings his legs out of the bunk. 'What would you have me do, sailor? Leave these people on the beach?'

'I don't think there's much point to this sort of talk,' I growl. 'If you believe that cramming a couple of hundred desperate people into a ship this size and taking them through a force ten storm is doing them a favour, there isn't much I can say to convince you.'

The grin fades. 'Listen, you supercilious bastard. This ship was meant to act only as a ferry; taking the immigrants from remote beaches out to bigger ships lying in deep water outside the three-mile limit. The ship I was supposed to meet did not rendezvous, and my guess is, your navy had something to do with that, so what gives you the right to lay down the rules?'

'No right at all – sir,' I stress sarcastically. 'It's just that I am not used to picking up messmates from small boats with bullet holes in their heads. Now – can we have some hot water please?'

'You're talking about Seddon.' He's a cold blooded sod: there's no sign of embarrassment on his face at all.

'Who else?' I sneer.

'Seddon was a plant. I'm not going to defend my actions to you, sailor. Remember, though, as far as those who hired me are concerned they are at war with the British Navy and he was a spy. They did what they reckoned was right when they executed him. As for me: I'm just a sea-going bus driver and I didn't even see it happen – you can believe what the hell you like.'

'Can I have the hot water?' I ask coldly.

'I would like to speak with your officer.'

'I'm only interested in water.'

'Take your bloody water!' he yells, suddenly losing control. 'Take it and get the hell out of my sight!'

*

There is a change in the wind and it is not just brought about by our new course. It is blustering in from the west, moaning through the rigging and tugging at my clothing. The moon rides ghostlike through a procession of heavy clouds, turning the night inky black beyond the halo of our lights when it hides behind them. I decide to go forward to check the tow and the men guarding it. As I go, the first cupful of growing sea comes inboard to wet my legs.

My thoughts are on the things Morgan said when I catch the glint of clean metal in the gloom beneath the break of the fo'c'sle, and a brief vision of a meat-cleaver flashes across my mind. I grab for the flap on my holster and my sudden movement is like a trigger to the man in the shadows. He leaps out at me with a wild yell before my revolver has cleared the holster, leaving me no choice but to try and dodge the cleaver, and the only way to go is over the side into the drink.

The Monday Mutiny

Weighed down with my boarding gear I seem to be going down forever, and there is a growing panic welling up in me as the pressure clamps my ears. My revolver is clear now and I let it sink as I flay desperately at the water. My boots are lead weights and my deflated lifebelt just a useless appendage. Only the air trapped in my clothing brings me back to the surface spluttering and gasping, grabbing for the mouthpiece to blow air into the belt. I'm still blowing when I go down again, but my head is clearing and I have sense enough to shut the valve. There is enough air to bring me up to the surface so that I can fully inflate the rubber ring.

For a while I can do no more than lie there and splutter. Regaining strength while the panic subsides. When I am recovered enough to look round the first thing I see is the lights of the two ships leaving me astern as they move away into a black void. I am utterly alone in the empty ocean and I choke back an involuntary cry as I watch them go.

My mind is beginning to function and I am thinking again; forcing my brain to reason out the situation as I tread water and spit out mouthfuls of brine. I circle slowly until I am facing the pin-pricks of light high on the cliffs. If I can see them from water-level they cannot be too far away. With a bit of perseverence there's a chance I can swim that far. No need to worry about keeping afloat, the rubber life-belt will take care of that, so all I have to do is keep pushing towards those lights. The distant rattle of automatic fire drifts down from the distant ships, but that is no longer any concern of mine. I have but one thing to concentrate on now, staying alive and pushing towards the shore.

There is no point in studying the lights for they will not change to give any comfort during my long swim. It will be long past daylight before I can hope to reach shore, so I occupy my mind with other thoughts and forget about time and distance. The wind and sea comes from behind to give an illusion of pushing me towards the shore. In reality my progress is infinitesimal – slower than the slowest walker – measured only by willpower and an inborn drive to stay alive. I can even summon up a chuckle when I recall that this is the second time I have been attacked with a meat-cleaver: there must be something about me that attracts maniacal butchers.

The small red light attached to the life-belt bobs energetically beside my head like my own personal little star, trying to comfort me in this wilderness. Home seems far away now. Home: where the hell is home for me? Certainly not the two-up two-down terrace house where I was born. Anywhere I hang my cap, I suppose. The Trafalgar Club in Pompey. The White Ensign Club in London. The brand new NAAFI in Plymouth maybe? I shut my eyes to that thought for it brings memories of a lovely face and the wicked little pout on sweet lips when she holds on to me. The pain comes when I think of her. There never was a person like her, and yet I pulled away. Jesus, I must be nuts! So certain I was doing the right thing for both of us. How could I know how much it would hurt? How hard it would be to push her image away?

I choke as my head is submerged by a rogue wave and it brings me back from those hopeless thoughts. My home is a couple of feet of hammock-rail in whichever ship I happen to serve; that's the hard, uncompromising truth. Ashore, especially in England, I am an alien, out of place amongst ordinary people, and that thought is the worst of all, for I know I have allowed the Navy to take me over body and soul.

My limbs are growing heavy now. The tiredness seeping into my aching bones. A couple of times I have felt objects slide past my body and assume they are seaweed or jellyfish, but my clothing protects me from stings. My boots weigh a ton. I would be much better off without them, but I am wearing gaiters and even if I could get them clear I doubt if I could loosen the laces. No, there's nothing to do but kick out and try to shake away the depression. I roll onto my back as though that will change the visions, but it is a mistake for stars mean distance – enormous, incalculable distance, and I know that as far as I am concerned the shore is just as unattainable.

My legs slump down, unwilling to thrust any more, and the listless movement of my arms will not influence my drift. I am a piece of flotsam, drifting aimlessly and there isn't a hope in hell that any power on earth will push me in the direction I wish to go. I feel a great surge of self-pity and an urge to weep as the visions come again. I see the face I will never see again in life, looking so desperate and sad.

Perhaps it is better that I should die out here. 'Lost at sea' they'll say. The way a sailor should go, but it brings small comfort now. I notice my head is ducking under more often. Reluctant to lift again, and it is a long time since I remembered to blow more air into my belt. Perhaps I shouldn't bother; it's only prolonging the agony.

Through the bluster I hear a new sound. A growing mutter like some approaching beast as it forages for food. I concentrate, trying to work out what strange creature could make that sound for there is no doubt it is coming for me because the noise grows until it seems to throb inside my body. Any second now great crunching jaws will close on me and there is no way of escape for my limbs are drained and useless. So I wait for it to come, too weak to extinguish my little red star that is guiding the beast towards me.

'I've got 'im,' says a voice, and the hard clinker-built flank of the motor-cutter looms above me as strong arms reach down to drag me inboard.

Six

Standing on *Condor*'s bridge I am amazed to learn that I have been in the drink for only thirty-five minutes and none the worse for my midnight swim. Dressed in clean togs and revived with a tot I am ready to face what comes, so the skipper obliges by telling me I have to go back to the immigrant ship again. This time Lieutenant Border is coming with me, and we are taking a quantity of watchcoats to keep the lads warm until the sun comes up.

My little affray with the cleaver-man churned up a bit of a rumpus that was subdued only after several shots were fired into the air, and the situation is more volatile now, prompting Subby to signal for a senior officer to assume responsibility now that the shooting has started. Meanwhile the ether is jumping and the radio spells out instructions to hold on to the ship. We must convince the immigrants that we are the only ship in their vicinity and therefore have a moral duty to stand by them and bring their stricken ship to safety.

'That's the situation,' states the captain bluntly. 'I am relying on you to see that there is no more gun-play unless it is absolutely unavoidable. Is that clear?'

Border answers for both of us and within ten minutes the cutter is back alongside the *Star of Judea*, and I feel the tension the moment I step on board her. The sea is rougher too, with waves washing over the low side. There is nothing to worry about yet, but if it gets worse we will have to batten down at least one of the two hatches. I make my way aft with the navigator and find Subby in the wheelhouse with Morgan.

The long watchcoats are handed out to the men who have to adjust their webbing to fit over the bulky garments. There seem fewer people on deck now, but that is probably because they are huddled into small groups in the shadows, looking conspiratorial as they mutter amongst themselves. I get the impression that the whole ship could erupt at any moment.

After a short conference with Subby, Border turns to me. 'I want you forward please, Coxswain. Take two extra men with you and try to ensure that Petty Officer Bold knows he must wait for my orders before his men open fire again.'

'With due respect, sir,' I put in quickly, 'I don't think he had time to wait for orders when that bloke attacked me.'

'That's just it!' exclaims Subby. 'No one fired then. Leading Seaman Henry and his men overpowered the man and locked him in one of the cabins. The firing took place elsewhere and was meant to distract attention from the disturbance. The men were ordered to fire into the air and it did have the effect of quietening things down. Under the circumstances I believe Bold was justified in giving the order. After all, a very ugly situation was developing. Nevertheless, I do not want a repetition, Grant. We have had only one casualty since we took over the ship and I wish it to stay that way.'

'There is one thing, sir,' says Subby. 'The immigrants have asked for a meeting and would like to send a delegation to negotiate.'

'All right,' agrees Border after a moment's thought. 'I cannot see any harm in that.'

'When should they come up, sir?'

'Sooner the better. Let's get it over with. Who knows, maybe we can persuade them to co-operate while we tow the ship to safety. How do we contact them?'

'Through their captain, sir. Incidentally his name's Morgan.'

The Monday Mutiny

Border looks over to where the master has withdrawn to stand on his own, brooding just outside the starboard door. 'Captain Morgan! That's an appropriate name – not very Jewish though.'

Morgan must have sharper ears than we think for he sticks his head inside the door. 'No, Lieutenant. I am from Bala in North Wales, and I'm no pirate either. Just trying to earn a crust with all the other thousands who have been put on the beach now we are no longer required.'

'Hm, well I'm not here to judge issues of that kind, but you can't blame our lads for their unfriendly attitude. They take a dim view of someone who is mixed up in the murder of one of their shipmates.' He takes a breath. 'Can you bring your delegation up here to us?'

'Not my delegation, Lieutenant. As I told you before; I'm just the driver. Give me five minutes.'

'Shall I go forward now, sir?' I ask when he's gone.

'No, not yet, Coxswain. Once you are on the fo'c'sle you will be cut off from us and I want you to know the full score. If we do persuade them to co-operate you might have some extra help up there. It is in their own interest to help us to get their ship safely into port, although I doubt if they'll see it that way.'

Two men accompany Morgan when he returns and they are complete contrasts. One is in his early twenties wearing only a thin cotton shirt with rolled-up sleeves in spite of the cold, looking full of fire and brimstone with his dark eyes flashing dangerously as he follows his mate. The leader seems determined to keep the younger man safely tucked away behind him. He is middle-aged, stolidly built, with steel-grey hair thatching heavy features, and his eyes are deep-set with lines radiating from the corners. They are the eyes of someone who has suffered a long illness and knows he will never be rid of its ravages.

He is the quiet one, yet holds the authority and seems to command respect amongst the Jews – even the hot-headed youngsters. He will weigh each word and mollify his more extreme comrade while we talk. He will be a hard man to bargain with, and he will gain more in the long run than those with fire in their bellies and empty heads. When he speaks it is with a thick East European accent and one feels he is a man to trust.

'These people have tiredness and some have illness. We wish to know where you are taking us.'

'We are towing you to safety.' Border spaces out each word. 'You will be well fed and looked after. Your sick will be treated by doctors. We wish you no harm.'

He takes time to absorb what Border says. Making sure he has fully understood before attempting to reply. 'For some there is little time. They have very bad illness. Soon they may die.'

Border leans forward sympathetically. 'I'm sorry. We shall do all we can for them.'

This brings a stream of outrage from the youngster who waves his arms about wildly, spitting out abuse as he remonstrates with the older man. Finally he points a thick, accusing finger straight at Border. 'This is open sea, Englishman. You have no right to board us here.'

He rants on while the older man tries to placate him, and one of our leading hands cocks his sten and lowers the barrel.

'Hold it!' I bark urgently. 'Put up that weapon!'

It has a sobering effect on the youngster, and allows his mate to get in a few words. We wait while they argue.

'Keep your people under control and there will be no trouble,' Border urges when the argument dies. 'It will be better for everyone if you help us to get this ship into harbour.'

'Where?' demands the youngster aggressively.

Border looks uncomfortable. 'You will find that out when we get there, and that is all you need to know.' He turns to the older man. 'I suggest that you go and tell your people we mean them no harm, and try to restrain your friend and his like before they instigate something that will lead to disaster.'

For a moment they stand looking at us: full of doubt and anger. Their minds working over the implications as they try to read what is in Border's promises.

'That's all,' insists the navigator, nodding towards the ladder.

The older man looks at our seamen and the stens held across their chests and takes the youngster's arm to lead him away. I watch them go with a strange sort of compassion.

'All right, Grant. You can go forrard now,' says Border in a tired voice.

I drop down into the waist, picking my way carefully. I am wearing a submarine sweater under my uniform jacket and feeling a lot warmer as I mount the short ladder to the fo'c'sle. The ship is bouncing about a lot more now, and the cable is slamming down on the metal 'scotsman' with loud clanks that echo through the hull. We do not seem to move through the water at all, and when I lean to peer down at the stem there is not even a sliver of bow-wave. Only the tightening of the hawser as the slack is taken up shows we are still under tow.

'You have ter watch these crafty bastards,' snarls Bold's voice in my right ear. 'I can 'ear 'em scratchin' abaht dahn there, all secret-like, and I know the sods are up ter somethin'.'

'You just keep a tight rein on your men,' I warn him. 'We've had a word with their leaders, and providing they stay quiet and show no more aggression things should go smoothly. Don't wreck it all with a stupid move.'

'You believe them, do you?' he scoffs, leering at me. 'They are a mixed bag, Swain. Germans, Poles, Russians: you name it they're there. How can you trust a mob like that?'

'I'm not telling you to trust them. Watch them carefully by all means, but don't get trigger-happy.'

'I'll not risk any of my men – not for a crowd of fuckin' Jews,' he states bluntly.

'No one is asking you to for, Christ's sake!' I can feel him shaking with emotion. He is tensed up to breaking point, I know it. One spark will set him off and he will need to be watched more than the immigrants. I pat his arm consolingly to cool him down a bit. 'You're doing a good job, mate. Keep it up and we'll be rid of them by morning.'

He snorts disbelievingly and moves away, leaving me in my own small world right up in the bow, savouring the keen wind and watching *Condor*'s quarterdeck lights dancing ahead of us.

At eight bells Subby sends a relief party forward with Leading Seaman Henry in charge. I trust him more than Bold so I am happy to leave him watching over everything while I go aft to the wheelhouse for a break. The sea is boisterous now and *Condor* is having her work cut out to make any headway at all. Our helmsman is doing his best to make it easier for her, but despite his efforts the immigrant is yawing badly, swinging almost beam-on to the sea at times and the cable is snubbing hard at the fair-lead.

The immigrants are battened down in their fetid quarters with only one hatch in use. They must have learned their lesson during the storm because a couple of men are stationed there to regulate essential traffic as the gale increases, but even so the sea finds its way below to add to the misery. We all pray for daylight to come and hope the sloop will not find it more and more difficult to retain steerage-way and make the tow impossible. The one consolation for the Jews is that the wind is from the west, pushing us towards the Palestinian coast.

It is about five-thirty when Monday comes up from below. I had forgotten about him and his sudden appearance sours the atmosphere, for I just know he is going to bring another bloody problem.

'Swain!' he calls, looking about as he tries to locate me in the gloom.

'I'm over here.'

'The doctor sent me up. That pregnant woman – she has gone into labour and it looks complicated.'

The Monday Mutiny

'How's that?' Border comes forward from the rear of the wheelhouse and Monday switches to him gratefully. 'She's having a hell of a time, sir. The doctor says she should have a caesarean.'

'Good God!' Border is a married man with two children and I can almost hear his brain ticking over as he turns to look forward at the tow, thumping a fist on the wood capping as if to drive the solution into his head. 'We will have to move her into one of the cabins. I assume there is nowhere in the hold where the doctor can look at her properly?'

'No, sir.'

'No; well, get to work on it right away. You will need a stretcher-party won't you?'

'The immigrants can manage. They've had plenty of practice recently, but we will have to come through here. It is impossible to open the main-deck door, for it is on the port side and under water for much of the time.'

'You had better use the saloon.' Morgan interrupts from the darkness. 'It's bigger than the cabins and there is a water-heater in the pantry. The doctor can use the big table.'

The saloon runs the whole width of the ship directly beneath the wheelhouse, with square ports looking out across the cargo deck. With sheets spread over the big dining table it will make a reasonable operating theatre. Monday scuttles away again with the good news, only to return within a few minutes to say it is no good; the doctor says that without anaesthetic, blood and oxygen he won't operate. If the ship cannot make port within an hour or so all they can do is try to turn the baby and pray for nature to perform a miracle. They will take her to the saloon however – she'll find more peace and privacy there.

Border is glum. 'There isn't a chance of making port in an hour, or even two or three I'm afraid, Monday. The tow is becoming more and more difficult every minute as the weather deteriorates. I'm sorry, but the doctor must do the best he can with what he has.'

'Thank you, sir,' retorts Monday with heavy sarcasm. 'I'll tell that to the mother; she'll be thrilled to hear it.'

'That's enough!' I bark at him. 'Curb your tongue, Monday.'

'All right, Coxswain.' Border's palms are turned down as he tries to placate me. 'There's no point arguing amongst ourselves.' He turns to Monday. 'We will do our best, but remember, they have brought all this on themselves by refusing help from the Norwegian tanker. Quite frankly it was downright irresponsible to bring a pregnant woman on such a journey.'

The leading SBA chokes back his anger. 'It's just that she is so young, sir. Her husband is already in Palestine so she is going through all this without his support. It's a nightmare down there in the hold. We can't just let her die.'

The screaming begins a quarter of an hour later. Screams such as I have never heard that wrench at my soul. Agonised shrieks driving into my brain like hot irons even through the metal deck-plates. They pierce the night above the roar of the storm and those on deck turn their heads away as though that might lessen the sound. Everyone falls silent; locked into themselves, staring hardfaced into space, their minds numbed by someone else's pain.

At first there are blessed periods of quiet between bouts, but as time passes the intervals shorten until the air is continually filled with the awful sound. It seems impossible that the shrill cries can lift another octave, or gain in volume, but they do. When the climax comes I cringe with sweat pouring out of every pore, then mercifully the shrieks die to a heartbreaking groan and we are left with a terrible silence.

The quiet hangs heavy inside the wheelhouse, with only the creak of the helm and the moaning wind. The cold suddenly increases, knifing into my bones as the long minutes tick by, and we all tense for the next sound that must come from below. Everyone's thoughts are with the mother and child beneath our feet; each second seems a lifetime as we wait with our nerves stretched. When it comes I can't control a choked sob as the muted wail of a new-born baby lifts from below. Subby chuckles nervously, and there is a general shuffle as we relax our muscles.

'Who would have thought it!' breathes Morgan softly. 'In the midst of all this a new Israeli is born into the world.'

Dawn has arrived without announcing itself, taking us by surprise as it grows out of the east to put life into the grey ocean and reveal the two wallowing ships still shackled together on their endless journey. It sparkles on beads of dew hanging like pearls from the rigging and paints rainbows in the showers of spray that blow in from the west. It soaks up the damp patches on the iron deck outside the wheelhouse with trails of white vapour drifting up to evaporate in the warm air, and men peel off their watch-coats as they feel the sun.

'What the hell!' Morgan's voice shocks us all and we follow his gaze as he looks to starboard with an outraged expression on his face. 'We are not going to Haifa!' he accuses through clenched teeth.

All eyes turn towards Border as he tries in vain to hide his embarrassment. 'That's correct, captain. No one in authority ever said we were. Everyone just assumed so, and I saw no point in disclosing the truth in case some hot-headed so-and-so started something during the night. We are being towed to Famagusta.'

'Jesus Christ!' exclaims Morgan aghast. 'At three knots it will take us fifty hours or more; it's a hundred and fifty miles at least!'

'There is a naval tug on its way to us,' insists Border woodenly. 'She should be with us very soon now, and she will tow much faster.' He looks away from our accusing faces. 'I assure you, it's for the best.'

The news spreads quickly throughout the whole vessel. Jew and Gentile alike receive it with stunned disbelief. Fifty hours in this sea! They look to each other for re-assurance that this is only an empty rumour. A vicious story spread by someone with a warped sense of humour. Yet even I can see how much further away the coast is and how *Condor* is towing us at a tangent towards the north-west. Throughout the long hours of darkness the one dominating thought that sustained us was that with daylight would come relief and the quiet comfort of a safe haven in Haifa where the sick would be landed and nursed back to health after their ordeal. We hate every rivet in this ill-conceived bucket, and wish only to be rid of her rotten smells and miseries. No one has actually lied to anyone; they just didn't tell the truth.

Only the officers in *Condor* knew the awful truth until Border came across, and they were too nervous to tell even the boarding party in case it leaked to the Jews and caused a riot. Now the secret is out and we are faced with a new crisis. Those like me who have lived through the tensions of the long night and felt the suppressed hatred and anger have no doubt that there will be no holding the extremists now. They will never submit to being meekly towed away from their promised land; it's only a matter of time before we find out what they have in store for us.

'We're not much better than the Germans, are we?' spits Bunts. 'They played games with these poor bastards too: led them through false doors and treated them worse than animals.'

'You don't know the whole truth,' protests Border. 'There is a full alert in Haifa. The military are too busy to take care of another immigrant ship. We have no choice.' He turns to Morgan. 'You had better explain to them that any show of resistance will only jeopardise the safety of the people. Tell them to remain calm and all will be well.'

Morgan stares at him in disbelief. 'You want me to tell them all will be well when they know they have to endure two more days and nights in this hell!' He shakes his head violently. 'You tell them, Lieutenant. It's your problem now – you explain it all to them. Do it cautiously though, for you are sitting on a powder-keg. These people are sick of promises, and they've stared death in his face so long now he doesn't scare them any more. They are sick and tired of being pushed around, Lieutenant. One more hour is eternity to them now they have seen Palestine, and you think they will wait patiently for two more days!' He laughs ironically. 'I'll stand back here and watch; it should be quite something!'

He leaves us all swimming in a vacuum, knowing that the explosion must come, though in what form is anyone's guess. The immigrants are grouping in one big assembly, smack in the centre of the hatch-covers where they can argue without being overheard. Leading Seaman Henry and his small fo'c'sle party look down at the mob then lift their anxious eyes to us, and I realise they are probably the only ones in the ship who do not fully understand the situation. We dare not yell to them, and it's a cinch the Jews won't enlighten them. For one crazy moment I consider asking permission to go forward to them, but commonsense tells me I would not make it. The seething mass is just waiting for some idiot like me to come within arm's length. At best I would end up as a hostage; always supposing they spared my life.

The waist is a no-go area for us, and our men are spaced out at intervals in a line across the front of the bridge. Each man wears a holster with his .38 revolver, and carries a sten with a clip of twenty five rounds in the magazine. Their long coshes hang from lanyards on their hips for no one seriously pretends any more that it won't take more than coshes to quell what happens when the trouble begins.

Two weeks' special training in Malta is supposed to prepare them for this, but I doubt if any sort of training is sufficient to cope with this lot. It will be up to Border and Subby to make the right decisions as events develop, and for us NCOs to ensure the men carry out their orders to the letter. My eyes are drawn momentarily to Petty Officer Bold as he stands poised with his automatic held away from his body. His fingers are twitching on the weapon as he watches the shadows nervously, and I visualise his muscles taut under his action-working-dress. He is like a tightly coiled spring, and again the nagging worry gnaws at my guts.

For two hours it remains like that, with the tension growing every minute. The Jews move about stealthily without looking at us, and there is a great deal of whispering going on. It is a relief when one of our fo'c'sle party reports that the tug is in sight, coming down from the north with a big bone in her teeth. She blusters up to us, shouldering the sea aside like a busy little charlady. I had expected a big sea-going tug, but this one is small with a tall white and black funnel pouring out thick black smoke, and rust oozing from every seam. She is no slouch at her job though, and she moves in professionally to take over the tow.

Even in this weather her crew put their big hawser on board in quick time with the eye firmly placed over our bollards. *Condor*'s wire is cast off and hauled in as she threshes ahead to get out of the tug's way, and we notice an improvement right away. It seems this bucket recognises an expert when she sees one and comes to heel obediently. For one thing the tow is much shorter now, allowing her little chance to yaw. Each time she tries to pay off a point or so she is mercilessly yanked back on course like a naughty dog. We need to do little more than hold the helm amidships as the speed of the tow builds up to a steady five knots, effectively cutting the towing time to thirty hours or so. The news is conveyed to the immigrants, but falls on deaf ears. There is something brewing down there and their only concern is that we are heading away from Palestine to yet another internment camp. Hostility simmers down there like a devil's brew, stretching our nerves as we watch.

Condor circles to take station on our port side, watching over us like a mother hen. She is a comfort to us, for we feel less isolated with her standing by. After another uneventful hour we begin to concentrate on the weather more than the

Jews, for it seems to hold more menace as the storm increases and we lose sight of the coast. It will be twenty odd hours before we can hope to sight the coast of Cyprus, and except for the three ships the sea is empty. It is hard to realise we are moving at all for the circle of vacant wilderness appears to stay with us as if we are confined to this sad area of ocean.

There is nothing we can do for the immigrants in the hold now, and it isn't long before they begin to suffer again as the ship is tossed about on the end of her tow. The tug is powerful enough to jerk the bows into line when she begins to wander, sending shock-waves through the hull and increasing the nauseous sensation for those already suffering below.

I close my mind to the misery down there and take a spell on the wheel. It would be simple to keep the rudder amidships, and that is exactly what we order the less experienced helmsmen to do, for they can do more harm than good if they are left to experiment. With a little skill and anticipation however, it is possible to help the tow by keeping the two ships in line astern, gaining that invaluable half knot of extra speed. It is a work of art watching the big rollers come in from the port bow to take hold of the little tug and lift her bodily so that she see-saws over the crest and hoists her squat stern into the air before taking a dive into the trough beyond.

The same wave advances on us, bent on pushing our blunt bow to starboard so that the tow is oblique, dragging the tug's stern over with the hawser at a tangent, stretched to breaking point. At four knots our rudder has bite and a tiny bit of helm will hold our bow into the throat of the wave to stop the swing. It takes the strain off the hawser and we do not lose so much way. It needs to be judged exactly right or we can botch it and make things worse, so only those with the skill and experience are allowed to try it, and that means myself and Able Seaman Dobwell who has been hauled protesting out of his paint-store to take part in the boarding.

Not for nothing does he wear three red badges on his sleeve – he has never been known to buy gold ones – and when he takes hold of the wheel miracles seem to occur. I pride myself on my own prowess at the helm, but I have to acknowledge this maestro is the better helmsman. Even the impassive Captain Morgan is impressed when the disreputable AB takes the wheel.

I need to study the sea carefully, watching the way the rollers build as they converge, for no two are the same and I must wait until the very last moment before I dare put the wheel over. Not Dobwell: he stands there in is scruffy gear chewing away with his stubbled chin rotating, seemingly totally uninterested in what the sea has to offer, yet his hands are never still. They caress the spokes like a lover caresses a woman, and the wheel seems to spin of its own volition. On one occasion when the bow lifts to blot out the tug and a body of solid water hurtles out of the gloom he seems oblivious to it, wearing a glazed expression as though his mind is miles away, and I'm on the point of wrenching the wheel out of his hands as he absentmindedly spins it in what I consider to be the wrong direction, only to see the bow descend with the hawser straight and lined up with the two ships as though the wave had never existed.

I make a mental note. These skills are too valuable to be ignored, and Dobwell's halcyon days are numbered. Someone else will mix the paint in future and the disgruntled old stripey will begin watch-keeping as a quartermaster – a victim of his own expertise.

The starboard door bursts open and Monday is there looking tired and anxious. 'The mother is very ill,' he says. 'The doctor says she may not live unless we get her to hospital quickly. I have heard a rumour that we are not going to Haifa and it is going to take fifty hours to reach Famagusta.'

'It's no rumour, Monday,' states Border firmly, 'and there's nothing to be done about it. If the sea was smoother we might have considered requesting a seaplane, but in this weather that is out of the question. Unless you know of any way she can be plucked out of the ship and flown ashore there is nothing to be said. Anyway, there is likely to be trouble with the immigrants and I want you up here where you belong. If there is fighting you will be required to attend to our own casualties.'

'The doctor needs all the help he can get. I am in no danger down there. They are all too busy nursing the sick to worry about me. The majority have had enough, sir, and I'm certain they would give no more trouble if only they knew we would alter course and head for Haifa. The few hot-heads wouldn't stand a chance.'

'You will remain here, Monday,' insists Border resolutely. 'That is an order.'

'But, sir!'

'Enough!' snaps Border. 'We have allowed you a lot of leeway. You are not to return below again without orders. Where's your cap for God's sake! You're supposed to be on duty.'

'Fuck my stupid cap!' Monday is beside himself, backing towards the ladder leading down to the saloon. 'I'm required below!'

He clambers down the rungs out of our sight, leaving us all stunned for a moment.

'Shall I go after him, sir?' I ask.

'No. Leave him. He will face the captain when this is all over, and if he persists with his insubordination he could be court-martialled, the idiot.'

'He's all of that, sir,' I agree, trying to ignore a deep feeling of sympathy that hides beneath my gruff words.

'*Condor* is signalling, sir.'

One of the men on the port wing is calling and beckoning towards the sloop as she wallows a couple of hundred yards away. She is having difficulty keeping station with us at this slow speed, and it looks as if she has had enough, for as the lamp flickers she increases revolutions to begin orbiting us. There will still be loads of broken crockery down in her mess-decks, and water slushing all over the place, but at least they will be infinitely more comfortable than the poor wretches in our hold.

The Monday Mutiny

The signalman shakes water off himself like a shaggy dog when he brings in the message. 'From *Condor*, sir. "Tug reports the tow becoming increasingly difficult – can maintain only three knots – please report conditions".'

Border ponders for a moment as we look down into the waist where the more resilient immigrants are huddled into groups on the high side. The sea constantly washes over the port rail so that the deck is permanently filled with turbulent water. The hatches are kept shut now, and the only air seeping down to the people in the hold is sucked through make-shift ventilators, and even these have their mouths turned away from the wind. The atmosphere must be like pea-soup.

I glance across at the navigator as he peers out into the mess. His face is haggard, as though he can see inside the hold and sense the condemnation in the hidden faces. It must be a living hell down there, and the thought of two more days and nights of this must be a nightmare. Especially when most of them know that a turn to starboard could bring relief to their suffering within a couple of hours.

'What about it, captain?' asks Border eventually. 'How much more of this can your ship take?' He looks almost pleadingly at Morgan, as though he is willing him to say his ship won't last, for that would get him off the hook. There would be no choice left to *Condor*'s captain other than to order an immediate turn for safety.

Morgan has no intention whatever of making it that easy. He wears a cynical half-smile as he looks at Border; gloating over the tortured indecision written in the navigator's expression. 'She isn't going to sink, if that's what you're asking: not unless it gets a lot worse. The hold is well sealed and the ship is like a submarine, so there is no danger of foundering. Your conscience is clear on that account, Lieutenant. It really adds up to whether you and your superiors can live with what you are inflicting on those poor devils, doesn't it?'

Border glares at him and I look away to where the small group of our fo'c'sle party are having a hard time holding on while the ship throws them about. Constantly drenched and cut off from their mates they must feel threatened by the gale and by the growing menace in the waist.

'Make to *Condor*: Have many sick – some serious – Require urgent medical aid – no immediate danger of sinking – conditions appalling.'

It is a long interval before anything happens, while the sloop slowly circles us. All eyes are focused on her as we wait for the lamp to flash a message that tells us to head for Haifa. The Jews are convinced that this new activity can only mean a change of heart, and already there is a stirring on the upper-deck as hope-filled eyes watch for the light to spell out salvation. They know as we do that even a change of course will bring moderation to the continual battering, when we are running with the sea. It will ease pressure on the tow and give the tug a chance to increase speed. To them it is plain merciful commonsense. No one really doubts that we are about to alter course, and at last the signal is stuttering a message.

'Well?' demands Border, the strain showing in his voice.

The signalman hands him the pad without speaking. Border reads it through slowly, then goes back over it a second time as though he cannot believe what he is reading, and a sudden surge of anxiety runs through me when I see his jaw tighten grimly.

'What does it say?' asks Morgan impatiently.

Border looks at him, his features heavy with despair. 'There is help on the way,' he says in a thick voice, as if the words are sticking in his throat. 'A destroyer is coming down from Cyprus in company with a larger tug, to help tow us into Famagusta.'

The silence in the wheelhouse seems to emphasize the sound of the storm as the wind blusters about the superstructure.

'The idiots!' grates Morgan through clenched teeth.

'They are playing with people's lives. Are you going to tell the immigrants, or am I?'

'Tell them what?' asks Border.

'For God's sake, man!' thunders Morgan. 'They think they're going to Haifa!'

'I can't help what they think. There has been no change in the orders, captain. What possible good will it do to make futile announcements?'

'Have it your own way,' sighs Morgan resignedly. 'They will learn the truth soon enough, and then watch out. They'll take you and your men apart; and who can blame them?'

Border turns to Subby. 'I must go outside, Sub. I should be with the men now. The fo'c'sle party should not be left with only Leading Seaman Henry in charge. Do you think you could negotiate the waist and get to them? We will cover you from here of course, but it will be dodgy I'm afraid. Say if you think it impossible, I won't hold it against you.'

Subby doesn't hesitate. 'I'll try to make it look as though I am the bearer of good tidings, sir. They might think we are preparing to alter course for Palestine.'

'Try to smile,' advises Morgan sardonically. 'They will pick your bones if they realise they are being fooled.'

They ignore him and Border turns to me. 'I'm going to leave you in here with Dobwell, Grant. When we are gone you will latch both doors and keep them latched until further orders – is that understood?'

'Aye aye, sir.'

'Right. Now, Captain. Do I have to lock you in your cabin, or can I trust you?'

'My only concern is for my ship, Lieutenant. The immigrants are your responsibility. Nothing I do will affect them, so you may depend on me to stay out of it.' He nods towards me. 'Anyway, your coxswain and I have an understanding.'

Border raises his eyebrows at me and I shrug to show I don't understand what he means either.

The wind rushes in as they go out, flipping the pages of the

The Monday Mutiny

signal-pad and skirling about our legs to clutch at our trousers with impish talons. The heads and shoulders of the seamen stationed across the fore-part of the poop show above the wheelhouse ledge, and even though their faces are turned away and concealed beneath their helmets I can recognise most of them from the set of their shoulders. Most are very young. Caught up in something they do not fully understand. They will be feeling nervous as they look down into the milling mob and it will take a strong, self-assured man to keep them in order.

Border and Subby meet those requirements, but it will be Petty Officer Bold who relays the orders and who is closer to them, for he has been in charge from the outset. They look to him for guidance, and he is the man who saw them through their training in Malta. They must trust his judgement even though he is only Border's mouthpiece, and that thought fills me with trepidation when I look over to where he crouches with drooped shoulders and one arm wrapped round a stanchion in the port corner of the wing while he clutches his revolver in the other.

His face is set in a tight mask with a glint of madness in his wild eyes that only I can see, for he is hidden from Border and too far away to communicate. The navigator is too busy to notice or maybe he would ensure they were within range of each other; then he would see the madness as I do, and recognise the latent menace that lies beneath it.

I can leave the helm to Dobwell and go to the front of the wheelhouse to look between the men's shoulders. The faces of the immigrants are turned towards me, watching suspiciously as Subby makes his way down the port ladder. When he reaches the waist they crowd in on him, pumping questions as he struggles forward knee-deep in sluicing water. He tries not to come into contact with them, making no response to their insistent shouting. He has to move from handhold to handhold, staying deep in the water to keep clear of them.

As yet they are holding themselves in check, half

The Monday Mutiny

convinced that he is on his way to make preparations to alter course. Most have little or no English, and the only words that come through to me are 'Haifa' and 'Palestine'. Subby keeps shaking his head at them, pretending not to understand, and he almost makes the fo'c'sle when suddenly a clarion cry lifts above the hubbub. The thin, piping shout of a boy no more than twelve or thirteen years old who prances like a demon in front of Subby, moving easily to the swing of the ship while the sea washes up over his spindly legs.

Subby cannot shake this lad away for he speaks good English, and he and his small gang of followers bar the way to the fo'c'sle ladder, making it clear that the officer is not to be allowed forward until they have an answer.

Subby stays dumb, shrugging his shoulders and nodding towards the bridge, fooling no one with his show of ignorance. They will not be put off any longer and I notice Border easing himself through the line of seamen to take his stance at the top of the starboard ladder where he can see them all. A volcano is on the point of erupting. One wrong move or ill-considered word will set it off.

'Everyone must stay calm,' he warns in a loud, steady voice. 'We can do nothing until my officer is on the fo'c'sle. Let him through and I will explain our intentions.'

'Why not tell us now?' shrieks the youth's strident voice. 'If we are going to Palestine why can you not tell us now? For the sake of the sick we need to know.' He is being prompted by the thick-set man who came to see us, and now stands a couple of feet away from the lad.

Border contemplates them for a moment while he contains himself. There is no emotion on his face, and I exchange looks with Morgan who just shrugs obliquely. Border raises his voice. 'You allowed us on board to help save your ship. You must let us proceed with the tow in the best way possible. If you don't you are in danger of sinking. Believe me, it is in your interest to let us get on with the job. Allow my officer through – I will not be intimidated.'

The youth's translation causes a ripple of argument amongst the others, and everyone starts putting his oar in. Subby remains impassive and gaunt, facing the crowd of menacing men who stand between him and the ladder. His position is precarious and he is depending on Border now, praying that he will say the right thing and resolve this stalemate.

They seem to reach an agreement, for several of the senior men approach the youngster and talk to him with urgent gestures while he nods impatiently. Everyone seems to be speaking at once until he raises his arms and shouts at them to stop. When they have calmed down it is the thickset man who dictates the words he must use.

'We have been put off too many times already, Englishman. You must tell us now. We promise to let your officer go whatever you say.'

Border's eyes wander over them, and they stare back uncompromisingly as he speaks. 'There has been trouble in Haifa. A ship has been blown up by frogmen in the harbour and nothing is sailing in or out of the port. There has also been air activity over Tel Aviv, so the whole coast is on full alert. I do not have to explain what will happen if Arab aircraft catch this ship before we can get you to safety. It would be wholesale slaughter.'

He takes a breath before going on with a slight catch in his voice. 'Therefore, it has been decided to proceed to Famagusta where there are good facilities for looking after the sick and you will all be taken into care. The camps there are run by your people and I can assure you we have no wish to detain you for a moment longer than absolutely necessary for your own well-being.'

For a moment the only sound is the roar of the gale, then another roar swells from the belly of the ship. A noise that sends a thrill of alarm through me. It is an angry sound, like that of a monster who has been tortured until he is mad with pain. Subby makes a desperate effort to reach the ladder but promises are forgotten in this swelling tide of

The Monday Mutiny

outrage and they fall on him with flaying arms. Border draws his revolver from its holster and fires three shots into the air.

The mob freezes. Those who attacked Subby sprawl in a heap on his inert body and the thickset man, along with several others, begin to pull the youngsters away to leave the lean, unconscious torso face down in the swirling water. Two of *Condor*'s seamen clamber down from the fo'c'sle and lift Subby clear, placing him on the smooth surface of the hatch-cover. Sullenly the crowd pulls back into a circle while the boy who speaks English turns his bleeding face towards us.

'You did this!' he cries, his face twisted in shock. 'If he is dead you killed him!'

Border has sent two more men down into the waist and the immigrants back off to allow them through to help their mates.

'Where the hell is Monday?' yells someone. 'Subby's badly hurt by the look of him.' A figure is standing over the slumped officer waving his arm at us. ' 'E's bleedin' all over the place; fer Gawd's sake get the SBA!'

I swing towards the ladder and go clattering below. 'Monday!' I shout as I go, thumping down into the passage where two doors lead through the forward bulkhead. I wrench one open and find Monday with the doctor leaning over their patient.

'Monday!' I roar at him. 'Get up top at once. We have got an injured man!'

He turns to me. His face is defiant, and he makes no move to follow me out, just stands there staring at me with cold eyes.

'Did you hear what I said?' I thunder. 'You are wanted up top at once – get a bloody move on! Subby's badly injured!'

'Is he dying?'

I gape at him. 'What the hell has that got to do with it?' I gasp. 'Have you gone crazy or something? Get up there now – that's an order.'

He smiles a damn stupid smile while I stare in disbelief.

The Monday Mutiny

'There's two lives at stake here, Swain.' He deliberately turns his back on me as he goes on. 'The Navy doesn't own me any more, and I have no intention of leaving here. I have had a gutful of this stupidity.'

My mouth is opening and closing like a bloody goldfish. Completely at a loss I cannot think of anything to say as I back out into the passage, shaking my head as I clamber back up the ladder.

The situation up top hasn't changed. The immigrants are grouped together, uncertain of what to do next while our men stand with their weapons held across their chests staring down at them. Subby's torso is stretched out on the hatch and one of the seamen is bathing his face. 'How is he, sir?' I ask Border from the open door.

'Battered and bruised, but nothing worse, thank God. Where is Monday?'

I hesitate. God knows why I'm sticking my neck out for the idiot, but even now I am reluctant to shop him. 'He feels he cannot leave the mother and baby at the moment, sir. The old doctor needs him.'

He looks deep into my eyes. 'Did you order him up?'

Now I deliberately lie to him. 'I – I said I would see how seriously wounded Sub-Lieutenant Connault was first, seeing how desperately ill the mother and baby are, sir.'

He is about to say something when another shout comes from the waist. The crowd has moved aft to stand below the bridge, with the thickset man and his companions in front of them, all looking up at us. I hear the click of safety catches being eased as our men brace themselves.

'Steady!' warns Border in a heavy whisper. 'Watch them, Bold.'

I dart a glance at the GI's face and see his eyes focused on the mob, showing no sign of having heard or understood.

The ship takes a heavy roll, throwing many of the Jews off-balance into a tangled mess of arms and legs. It allows us time to return to our positions and I latch the door firmly. The ship stays slumped over with her port scuppers deeply awash for several seconds and I hear Morgan draw an anxious breath through his teeth as he feels the sickening motion. The immigrants pour up from below, oblivious of the danger they are causing to the ship as it begins to lose stability.

She plunges like a mad thing, unwilling to right herself after each violent roll to port as the additional top-weight destroys her stability. A few screams come when realisation dawns to some of the more nervous ones, and they struggle to climb to the high side. Morgan launches himself amongst them. Yelling, thumping, shaking in his effort to make them see what's happening. The list is increasing with every roll, making it almost impossible to keep a footing on the slippery deck. The weak cling to the strong, and the strong try to shake free, determined to get at our seamen. Like bundles of washing they are thrown about, and it is a miracle no one goes overboard.

Morgan fights his way through to the thickset man and the two of them set about restoring order amongst the rabble. Somehow our men have managed to drag Subby aft, and another sickening roll provides a short truce as everyone strives to hold on amidst a chorus of terrified shouts. At last they seem to be getting the message, but by the feel of her the ballast has shifted again, and unless she is brought under control she will roll right over. Morgan and his mate are urging the passengers to get down below again.

Panic is taking hold now, mixing with the venom and hate, as they feel the convulsions of the ship. Our men are using their boots and the butts of their stens to fight back the tide of immigrants who are trying to mount the poop ladders in their effort to reach the wheelhouse. It is a miracle that no one has opened fire yet, and I can hear Border's voice urging his men to stay calm.

More and more of the Jews are becoming aware of their predicament as the ship staggers drunkenly into another series of violent rolls and brings a new bedlam of discordant screams. The more able are desperately trying to restore some sort of order and persuade frightened, bewildered immigrants to go below again, but they are reluctant to face the terror of the hold and need to be physically pushed through the hatch against their will.

There is little order now, and all manner of conflicting forces are at work in the waist, ranging from abject terror to intense fury. Even if a man could raise his voice above the sound of the tumult he would find no listeners amongst the screaming, yelling throng. So there is no way of bringing sanity back into the situation. They mill about the waist, bent on saving their own skins or attacking our men, each one driven by his own motives in the midst of the madness.

As yet our men have kept them from the fo'c'sle, mainly because it is impossible to mount a concerted attack while sliding about with every movement of the ship. Border and Morgan are shouting at each other above the racket, and seem to be trying to sort something out between them; eventually they must have reached some kind of agreement for I notice Border calls to the nearest seaman and his message is relayed along the line until it reaches Bold.

It has to be a warning to the men to keep their nerves and hold their fire while the first man in the line fires a short burst over the heads of the mob in an effort to restore order. As soon as Border is certain his message has got through he nods to the first man who lifts his sten. The sharp staccato has an immediate effect. A shocked silence while all eyes swing aft to see what new tragedy has taken place.

Drenched, white-faced, they watch Morgan leave Border's side to climb up unto the bridge-rail, clutching a stanchion as he prepares to shout his message down to them.

They are willing to listen to him, for this is the man who has brought them all the way from Europe. Nursed the ship through terrible storms to get them this far. They trust him as much as they do their own kind, and now he stands above them like some Old Testament prophet about to lead

The Monday Mutiny

them to the promised land. A sustained quiet overcomes all as they wait for him to speak, and the ship herself seems to be holding her breath; wanting to hear what he has to offer.

Morgan opens his mouth to speak, but before he utters the first syllable a raucous burst of automatic fire sears the air as Petty Officer Bold empties his weapon into the mass. His face is a distorted maniacal mask as he screams his hate at them and fires until the twenty-five rounds are exhausted, then he waves the gun above his head, yelling for his men to follow as he scrambles down the port ladder to wade in amongst them.

A tremendous roar of rage erupts from the crowd as they struggle to get at him. He is overwhelmed as they rip into him. Tearing, punching, scratching; everyone trying to reach him while he fights back, yelling at them with blood streaming down his face as he swings his sten about. He goes down under a forest of flailing arms, and the tumbling mass swamps him. They fall in a heap, too incensed to realise they are sliding towards the scuppers and the hungry sea. They hang on the brink for a moment, oblivious to everything but their own blind fury until one man screams a warning and grabs desperately at the rail. They go over the side, the man clinging to his handhold for a second or so, then he is torn away, and once again a heavy silence descends on the ship.

The sea is washing the scuppers clean. A body rolls loose-limbed with the motion of the ship, and a figure doubles-up in agony against the side of the hatch. Yet another claws at the steel cover as he tries to drag his body up the slope with blood pouring from a wound in the small of his back. How many other victims of Bold's madness went over with him we cannot tell.

Seven

Bold's frenzied outburst is enough to shock everyone into a kind of nervous truce. Many of the immigrants have been driven up to the high side, clinging to every available handhold with the deck sloping steeply away beneath them towards the port scuppers where they have just seen three of their own kind swept overboard. The interlude allows reason to filter into the minds of others, and some of the more level-headed individuals get amongst their fellows to calm the panic-stricken and take the fire out of the aggressive.

The ship is behaving better now that the bulk of the immigrants have been coaxed back down below. She is not so reluctant to right herself after every roll to port. Tucked back into their bunks they curl up with their fear and pray in isolation for a swift end to their misery. Beneath the howling wind and abominable noises of the ocean there is an underlying, brooding suspense that stretches our nerves. In every corner conspiring shadows seem to lurk, waiting to creep out when our backs are turned to exercise their cunning.

I look towards the fo'c'sle where Leading Seaman Henry and his small band of seamen hang on tightly while their precarious little perch bounces about beneath them. As I watch Henry casts a forlorn look aft towards Border. He and his men must be feeling very much alone up there, but there is nothing we can do to ease his situation while the mob prevents anyone crossing the waist.

The Monday Mutiny

We can see groups forming again, and the thick-set man is very much in evidence as he rallies them all towards the centre of the hatches. They are the young and strong of both sexes, all wearing the same defiant expression. The leaders are strong-featured men in their mid-thirties, with shirtsleeves rolled up tightly over their biceps. Nearly all wear soft, peaked caps, as though it is a uniform. They balance easily against the movements of the ship, curbing the fiery tempers of the younger hotheads and forcing them to hold back while preparations are made. It is the first time they have shown themselves like this. Until now they have kept in the shadows, burying themselves amongst the crowd. The way they are coming out into the open is ominous and I feel the climax is near.

Border is still urging his men to stay calm as tension builds up. I remember suddenly that he has lost his PO. There are NCOs down in the engine-room but they cannot abandon their station, so I send Dobwell out to make up the number. The men respect him, and his three badges give him a certain air of authority. If Border uses his loaf he will use the old painter to keep the youngsters in check.

After he has gone I latch both doors. Besides me there are only two others in the wheelhouse; the signalman and Morgan, and we wait together with the air charged with suspense, wondering what the hell's going to happen next. We don't have long to wait for suddenly there is an uproar of wild shouts and I look down to see the young man with the mocking eyes and long, black hair emerge unto the deck waving an automatic above his head, acknowledging the applause.

A surge of cold fear runs through me when I remember that this man was locked in a cabin with two of our men on guard outside in the passage. The crowd are rising to him. His presence lifts even the most terrified out of their stupor as they join in the acclaim. His face is aglow with triumph as he pumps the gun above his head.

At last the cheers and hubbub subside. They tense and

wait for him to speak. Every eye is on him as he drags the English-speaking youngster to his side with a friendly hand.

'Who is he?' I ask Morgan.

'They call him Caleb,' he says quietly. 'I keep out of his way as much as possible. That won't be his real name, and I wouldn't like to hazard a guess at whether he is Hagana or Irgun, but one thing is certain, when he is around things start to happen. If he is Irgun watch out. They are the ones who think the Hagana are too restricted in the way they go about things, and the only way to achieve a new Israel is to take the fight to the enemy.

'Those boys have little respect for lives on either side. They believe force is what is needed and the more examples they can show of their determination the better. Believe me, a good disaster suits their needs to the letter, and can you think of a better set-up for a catastrophe than an overloaded old bucket like this with no engine? The only thing standing between them taking over the ship is that thin line of nervous youngsters lined up across the front of the bridge who are under orders not to use their weapons. This is ready-made for them, Ben. The whole world would come out on their side if there is a major tragedy here. Just pray for everyone's sake that this bloke is not Irgun.'

He lapses into silence as we stare out at the groups. They seem to have sorted themselves out properly now. The Old and weak are being shepherded below out of harm's way while the rebels gather together. Several are carrying guns and it is easy to guess where they got hold of some of them. My blood boils when I recall the two sentries we left below: each carrying a sten and a revolver – enough to arm four immigrants. We are making a lot of mistakes today, and inexperience is a poor excuse when our aim is to preserve life on both sides.

When the first attack comes the immigrants have it all their own way, for they are well organised. The bulk of them face aft to give cover for their mates as Caleb leads a sortie into the fo'c'sle. We look on helplessly and get a brief glimpse of Henry's anxious face as he looks to Border for permission to open fire. Our lads stand no chance against that mob and are quickly overwhelmed. Almost at once the bows pay off and I know the Jews have cast off the tow-line.

The ship seems to sense her sudden freedom and rolls away from the wind, falling into a deep trough as a fresh chorus of distress lifts out of the hold. Henry and his men are bundled roughly down the ladders into the waist before being dragged, punched and kicked down into the hold.

'Jesus Christ!' I curse. 'What will the bastards do to them now?'

'Nothing, if they behave themselves.' Monday's voice swings me round to face him as he stands between two tough-looking immigrants with sten-guns aimed at my guts.

'They will be okay so long as you don't do anything stupid.' I can see he is unarmed. If he thinks that excuses him from what goes on he's very much mistaken. I'll have his balls for this.

'You had better call Lieutenant Border in, Swain,' he says evenly. 'We have taken the ship over now, and the hawser will not be re-secured until we have his word that we are being towed to Palestine.'

'We!' I spit at him. 'You've decided to change sides then: you do know what that makes you, don't you?'

'Am I supposed to wilt at the mention of the word "traitor"? You seem to forget; I have been down there amongst them so don't start telling me to do my duty, for Christ's sake! This ship is outside the three mile limit. We had no right to board her. No one's fooled by all the bilge about rescuing her.' His words are contemptuous but I can see him shaking with emotion. The very mention of the word 'mutiny' can send a chill through a serviceman's blood and the enormity of what he is doing is crushing down on him. He staggers as the ship lurches heavily. Unleashed, she is a wild animal and there is a dead feeling to her as she cavorts to the whim of the ocean.

The Monday Mutiny

I have heard it said by experienced yachtsmen that one way to get out of a dangerous situation in heavy seas is to 'let-fly' and allow the boat to dance to the tune of the sea, so that she can find her natural movement without the false influence of sail or propeller. Well that theory is being put to the test now, and I don't reckon much to it.

Muffled cries of alarm come from the waist, and there is a desperate shout as someone is wrenched away from his handhold to slide down the sloping hatch-cover. He must have been missed when they sent all the old and weak below for he is no more than skin and bone, a relic of the death camps. An ancient wretch thrashing about hopelessly as he slithers toward the hungry sea without a sound. It is as though he sees no point in struggling to stay alive anymore. His white face is turned towards me and I can see his eyes sunk deep into his skull, and his mouth is a toothless cavern as it gapes open in a silent scream. He is a bag of bones, no longer willing to fight, accepting what fate holds in store.

They go after him, grabbing his weak arms and loose clothing to haul him back to the upper side of the deck. He is like a rag doll when they hand him over to others to coax down below into the waiting arms that reach out of the hold. His rickety old frame disappears into a welter of noise and shadows.

Now the ship is behaving like a deranged animal as she struggles on her beam-ends. She slews helplessly while everyone hangs on and prays for her to come upright again. She lifts reluctantly with a wild, swooping motion to poise squirming on the crest of a huge wave before plunging down in a sickening dive into the body of the trough. Juddering, vibrating as the sea thunders in over the port side to swirl through the legs of the people there.

'This is no way to help them, is it?' I shout at Monday, when I get a breath. 'How long do you think we can last like this, you stupid bastard?'

He makes a brave effort to hide his anxiety. The mad

antics of the ship are beyond anything we have ever experienced. She was designed as a landing-craft with her sea-going qualities forfeit to the nature of her particular role. She is shallow-draughted and almost flat-bottomed, so that she can ride up unto a beach. Now she has additional superstructure built on, and a multitude of extra bodies crawling about her upper deck to make her even more top-heavy. The steel hatch-covers are all that save her from becoming swamped when she scoops tons of ocean with every roll to port.

'Get Lieutenant Border,' he says icily. 'We are wasting time.'

I nod across to the signalman who dodges out onto the starboard wing, and in a moment Border is inside with us, looking weather-beaten and bewildered. 'Is what this man tells me true?' His eyes are blazing.

'If he told you Monday has gone round the twist, sir, then the answer is yes. That's the only explanation I can find for this lot.'

'What about it, Monday?' The ship heaves again, throwing us hard against the nearest projections. I'm up fast, bracing to lunge at the two gunmen, but they recover even quicker and the chance is lost.

'If you do not turn this ship towards Palestine there will be a bloodbath, sir. We have a dying woman in the saloon. She won't live to see Famagusta. In the name of humanity we must alter course.'

'Haifa is out. You heard what I told the immigrants.'

'We are not talking about Haifa.' There is a dangerous edge to his voice as he goes on. 'This ship must head for the coast. She is built for beaching so it should not be too difficult to run her ashore.'

'My God!' thunders Border, taking a step towards Monday, only to bring up short as the two automatics lunge at his chest. 'Just what the hell do you think you are doing?'

The SBA looks uncomfortable for a second or so, then

recovers. 'I have to follow my conscience, sir. I don't think we have the right to interfere with these people. They will have enough to contend with when they get ashore and come to grips with the Arab terrorists.'

'What about Jewish terrorists?' I shout at him. 'Whose bloody country is it anyway? The Arabs have been there for thousands of years: they've got deeper roots than most English people can brag about. Would you be willing to hand over Cornwall or Yorkshire? What bloody right have they to just walk in and set up their regime in someone else's country?'

'Because they have no country of their own. Because no one will allow them to exist anywhere else. Because they've suffered more than any other nation, and because someone made them a promise when promises were cheap and Jews were needed to fight a bloody war.' He yells straight at me.

'You've been got at.'

'Be quiet, both of you!' snaps Border. 'Politics are no part of your concern, Monday. It isn't for you to work out the rights and wrongs of what you are ordered to do.'

Monday's face is working furiously. 'I can't help having a mind of my own, sir. Mine tells me that what we are doing is wrong. The two sentries feel the same way I do. They have given up their weapons. Like me they want no part in this. It is a matter of conscience, sir.'

Border's voice grows cold and threatening. 'I hope you realise what you are about, Monday. This is incitement to mutiny: the most serious charge a serviceman can face. If you stop this nonsense at once I can reduce it to "direct disobedience of an order", and that's serious enough. Mutiny carries a death penalty, so think hard; you will get no second chance.'

Monday draws himself upright to stare defiantly at Border. 'I promise you, sir. With or without me the Jews will resist until the ship sinks. I will remind you that already one Jewish immigrant ship has blown herself up with many casualties. These people have no life left now, except in Palestine. They won't crack, sir. Don't underestimate them. They have come too far to be put off now.'

The whoop of a siren breaks through the tension as a 'C' Class destroyer lifts her long, lean shape over the crest of a swell close to our port side. She shows twenty feet of keel when she breasts the ridge and pivots to smash down with a huge explosion of white spray. Sleek and powerful she makes *Condor* look like a workhorse, and I see by her pennant numbers her name is *Cheetah*. She looks dramatic, but anyone trying to negotiate her upper deck between the break of her fo'c'sle and her stern will need lifelines to run the gauntlet of the heavy seas washing inboard over her low freeboard. One day shipbuilders will find light alloys to replace the heavy steel and change the shape of destroyers for all time, making it possible for men to move fore and aft in the severest conditions without even getting wet, and those with memories of Russian convoys will bless them for it. Meanwhile white water spills over her torpedo tubes and streams out of her scuppers as her big twenty-one inch light spells out a signal to us.

Not surprisingly she wants to know what the hell is going on. Her skipper is a full-blown commander and that makes him senior officer, so now we have another man in charge. I can see her boarding-party fully kitted out and mustered on 'B' gun deck staring over at us. They will not be looking forward to leaping across in these seas while the old tramp buckets about like this.

'Englishman!' The youth is shouting again. They have hell's own job keeping their feet down there, but Caleb and his small companion do better than most as they stand with their mates staring defiantly at our men. 'Englishman!'

'Answer him,' demands Monday curtly.

'By Christ you're in it up to your neck now, laddie,' I think as I see the nerves jumping in his neck. 'You stupid oaf, they will lock you up and throw away the key when this is all over; always supposing they don't shoot you.'

The Monday Mutiny

Border leans out of the front of the wheelhouse. 'Well?' he asks harshly.

The ship throws herself into another series of wild antics and more pathetic noises lift out of the hold. The lad struggles to stay upright with water streaming down his face. 'You must tell them we go to Palestine. You must say we have hostages, and this new ship is not to come close.'

Border stares down at them for a moment. 'Hostages?' he queries with a catch in his voice.

The immigrants draw aside to reveal a group of our own men squatting on the hatch-cover. Leading Seaman Henry is there with his fo'c'sle party, and so is the Chief ERA, a stoker PO, and the men who went below to start the engine. I notice that there is no sign of the sentries who were guarding the cabins.

'These are our hostages, Englishman.'

Border studies them for a minute or so before turning to Monday. 'You can still salvage something out of this mess and redeem yourself to some measure if you have a mind. Remember, those are your shipmates down there.' He chooses his words carefully, as though each one holds the balance between life and death. 'If you have any influence with your new-found friends tell them we are not in the business of persecuting Jews. This ship is in dire trouble if we are not allowed to take her in tow. Tell them I will not carry out negotiations like this.' He takes a breath before continuing with a new edge to his voice. 'I will do nothing while he threatens the life of one of my sailors. However, if their leaders wish to talk again they can come up to the bridge.'

Monday glances at his two companions who are aiming their weapons at Border's stomach. 'You are hardly in a position to dictate terms, sir.'

The navigator's face is grim. He looks gaunt as he calls through the open door without taking his eyes from Monday. 'Dobwell!'

'Sir!'

'You are senior man out there. Your men will open fire on the immigrants if there is one move to harm any of our men – is that clear?'

The old seaman gulps and stares at us for a brief moment before he growls, 'Aye aye, sir.' Poor old stripey, the two rules he has always stood by are: never volunteer and never take on responsibility.

'Now, Monday. The ball is in your court. What do you intend to do with it?'

Monday considers for a second or so, looking from Border to me and seeing the same determination in both our faces. He knows full well we are not going to back down. We will give in to no one; least of all a bloody turncoat. This is costing him dearly. The sweat is pouring down his face, plastering his hair, running in rivulets through the stubble on his chin, and soaking darkly into his shirt, despite the way the storm keeps the day cool for the rest of us. There is no going back for him now. He is totally committed, and it is burning his insides.

'I'll take your message down,' he agrees in a thick voice.

'Good.' Border relaxes a little. 'Signalman; make to *Cheetah*: Negotiating under threat – situation in hand but delicate – please do not attempt to board.'

By the time bunts has passed the signal Caleb and the youngster are inside the wheelhouse, but there is no sign of the thickset man. The immigrant leader's eyes are even more intense. He doesn't speak, but nods to Border to start. The navigator speaks slowly, allowing the youth plenty of time to translate.

'There has been too much bloodshed already. No one is going to gain anything unless an agreement is reached. Tell me exactly what you want and I will pass it on. Before I do though, I want my men released.'

He must know there is small chance of Caleb agreeing to that, but it is worth a try.

The Jew shakes his head slowly as he listens to the translation. 'They stay with us. We will shoot them if the ships come near.'

'All right, then tell us what you want, and who you represent. Are you Hagana?'

'Hagana!' Caleb spits venomously over the side at the mention of the word. He thumps his chest. 'Irgun!'

My insides sink, so that is why the older man has not come up. This bloke's a fanatic; it shows in every tense muscle of his body. I dread to think what would happen now if this ship had power and was able to take avoiding action. The lives of the poor bastards below mean very little to Caleb and his mates. They are driven by hate, and the cause they give lip-service to is only an excuse to vent that hatred on the British, or anyone else who stands in their way.

Border's mouth tightens grimly: 'Signalman; make to *Cheetah*: Immigrant leader is Irgun – he holds several of our men – demands tow to Palestine coast – situation stalemate.'

The boy translates slowly and Caleb nods acceptance at the end of each phrase. Afterwards we all wait.

The ship throws herself about as though she is incensed by the delay. The noises from below are more subdued as the Jews become too exhausted to scream or protest anymore. They accept the battering with a sort of numbed apathy. Some would even welcome death if he would bring relief from their torment. She is a rolling hulk with a bellyful of agonised humanity who have escaped one hell for another. Now it seems, their future is in the hands of angry men.

There is no relief from their suffering as they live out the hours in the pale yellow light that emphasizes the crinkles and the strain on their stricken faces. Their claustrophobic dungeon reeks with the stink of vomit so that even to breathe is torture. Their debilitated bodies roll in harmony with her; bruising against the hard edges of their make-shift bunks. Others lie prostrate in the filth that slushes from side to side with every movement of the ship. The majority of them have no more will to fight. Their eyes are dull with the agony of retching on empty stomachs, and their skin is the colour of dirty parchment. They groan in unison when she heaves over until they cling almost without thinking to keep from tumbling out of their bunks. The few who are not sick have given up the struggle to help their fellows, for when someone no longer wishes to live there is little more to do. Any attempt to clean up the mess is thwarted by the violent antics of the ship.

After a long while the signalman returns to Border with his pad. *Condor* and the destroyer keep circling slowly while the little tug stands off to starboard. There is no sign yet of the larger tug that is supposed to have left Cyprus with *Cheetah*, but that's hardly surprising for the destroyer has three times her speed. Border reads through the signal slowly before looking up at Caleb.

'It's a compromise,' he says at last. 'I'll read you what it says. "Force nine to ten gales forecast – if immigrants comply and surrender arms their ship will be towed to Palestine – Hagana representatives and army will meet them – immigrants will be taken to Haifa by road."'

Caleb studies the navigator's face as the words are translated. He shows no emotion, and I can almost hear his brain working out the implications. As though to emphasize his predicament the ship is hit by a sudden squall that slams into her side and lays her over so far I swear the port wing dips into the water. Strangely enough, I'm too bloody tired to be scared anymore. Every muscle in my body is aching with the strain of hanging on against her insane convulsions.

'We will not surrender the weapons,' interprets the youth.

Border's eyes blaze. 'Then you put the lives of everyone at risk. This ship cannot ride out a force ten storm, and you cannot win in the end because whatever you do to us those ships will have to board eventually. We are offering all we can.'

The Monday Mutiny

Caleb shakes his head. 'No surrender.'

Border slaps his thigh in exasperation. 'In that case there is nothing to be done. With the weather deteriorating it will be difficult to attach the tow – soon it will be impossible. I will not risk my men on the fo'c'sle while your people are waving guns behind their backs.'

Monday chimes in, 'You've got what you asked for, Caleb. Why don't you put it to the others and see what they say?' He recoils as every eye focuses on him viciously. No one, not even those he has chosen to change sides for, have any time for him now.

For a moment the Jew struggles with indecision, then he looks at Monday and mutters something almost beneath his breath. The youth translates in a subdued voice. 'We will go down while you keep watch here with our two men.' The look in Caleb's eyes is merciless. I don't reckon much to Monday's future with his new-found friend, and there's no changing sides for him now.

The sky has become overcast. All traces of blue have gone and heavy cloud drives in from the west to cloak the world with its oppressive gloom. It seems even more doom-laden because it is so out of character in these parts. The old cynicism 'it never gets rough in the Med' comes back to me and I smile wryly. The sea is boiling up all the time and I expect we are getting the backlash from the lee shore. Getting a hawser secured is going to be a pig of a job even without the thought of these renegades roaming about behind us with weapons cocked.

The ship is lying broadside to wind and sea now, with every sign of staying there. Her waist is awash for most of the time and she must be shipping lots of water despite the metal hatch-covers. Some of the immigrants have climbed up to the fo'c'sle, but most are still huddled into corners where the superstructure offers a little shelter. Even the most ardent rebel looks half drowned and dejected now. The weather overpowers everything, so that survival becomes the main concern of all, even Caleb's followers.

He gathers them into a small group where they argue with a lot of arm waving and gesticulation. The seas crash in on them to interrupt their talk and I wonder if they are trying to prove something by enduring all that. No sane seaman would attempt to work down there in these conditions. Let alone hold a bloody meeting. Incredibly they survive and Caleb comes staggering aft with his hair strung out like rats' tails and water streaming down his body.

'The men are worried,' interprets the lad. 'The Hagana will not support us. They go their way and we go ours; it has always been so. The British are hanging Irgun in Palestine.'

Border has to shout above the noise of the storm. 'I know nothing about all that. The message states clearly that you will be towed to Palestine. What more do you expect?'

'Some guarantee for the safety of my followers and me.'

'I cannot offer you any more. It is not a case of what anyone will do to you when we reach shore, my friend. Just pray that someone will be there to meet us. We are going to need all the help we can get, for a lot of these people are too weak to help themselves. The odds are against us getting everyone ashore safely, and there is no chance at all unless you co-operate. I didn't read the full signal before, but in case you are in doubt about our position I will read it to you now.'

He takes up the pad and reads slowly; allowing plenty of time for the youth to translate. 'It goes on to say – if these terms are refused we will attempt to take off you and your men and abandon the ship.'

'You would leave us to die?'

Border sighs. 'You don't give us much choice. The ships will most likely stand by, but they will not take undue risks. There is no doubt at all in my own mind that if this ship founders there will be few survivors. Most will be trapped in the hold; others will drown before we can get to them.'

'There are rafts and lifeboats!' protests Caleb's interpreter off his own bat.

Border smirks. 'They are as good as useless. Do you believe that those doubled-up relics could be launched in these conditions? Refuse our help now and you condemn a lot of innocent people. Time is running out for you, Caleb. Martyrs will not build a new Israel.'

Caleb moves to stand looking out into the wild ocean with his hair streaming and the agony of his tortured thoughts showing in his face. He mutters a few sullen words to the youngster before turning and saying in English, 'We agree,' then hands me his automatic and dodges quickly out through the open door.

The youth starts to follow, hesitates, turns his head for a moment and says, 'Caleb said, "At least we will be in Palestine." ' He slaps the woodwork hard and goes off after his leader.

My watch says twelve thirty-five and it seems impossible that all this has taken place in the few hours since daybreak. Border sighs heavily before turning to me. 'It's up to you now, Coxswain. Take as many men as you require and go up to the fo'c'sle. Dobwell, you are now an acting, unpaid, temporary leading hand. You will collect the weapons and bring them aft to me. Take two men with you and try to make certain you get them all.'

Dobwell pulls a face behind Border's back as the navigator swings on Monday. 'What do you intend doing now that your friends have done with you?'

Monday looks grim. 'I must go below to help the doctor, sir. There is still a lot to do down there. After that – who knows?'

As he goes through the hatch I get that illogical surge of sympathy again. I know well enough that without his mutinous conduct we would most likely have held on to the ship and Caleb would still be locked in the cabin under guard. We would probably be halfway to Cyprus and some dead people would still be alive. Yet I have a grudging respect for the way he stood up for what he believed in. It took a lot of guts and I can understand his motive – however misguided. I shake the thought away and concentrate on the next problem.

'I can make do with Leading Seaman Henry and his team, sir,' I tell Border. 'The fo'c'sle is too small for more men than that, especially in this sea.'

He nods agreement and as I go down into the waist I see Dobwell and his mates gathering the weapons. They don't seem to be having any difficulty, in fact Caleb and his gang appear only too willing to assist now they have accepted the situation. When they receive the news that the ship is being towed to Palestine the immigrants make only a weak response. True there is a show of elation and triumph from some of the most ardent rebels, but mostly they are too weary or sick to care anymore. Even if a couple of weapons are missed it is not important. The main thing is that we can get on with the job without hindrance. The immigrants know their ordeal could end in a few hours if they co-operate, and they will have succeeded in reaching their promised land, but they have lived through a succession of false hopes. The time for rejoicing will come when their feet touch the soil of Palestine.

When I go forward amongst them I sense a new atmosphere. They avert their eyes or stare sullenly at me, but at least I do not get that nervous prickle in the middle of my back as I go by. Henry and his men show signs of their struggle with Caleb's gang; their faces bloodied and clothing torn. They're gutsy bastards, and more than ready to come back up to the fo'c'sle with me to get the tow rigged.

We stow our weapons in a small deck-locker and set about shepherding the immigrants down into the waist to clear the working area. Everyone is soaked through and we have to duck from time to time as hefty waves crash in over us. I am glad to find Stoker PO Mike Spiller there to work the winch. He is a young man for his rank, with a reputation for reliability and common sense. He and the ERA have kept the generator running throughout, and their efforts made the hellish conditions below a lot more tolerable during the long hours of darkness.

There is a tendency amongst the upper-deck brigade to forget these denizens of the engine-room. Their stolid devotion to duty earns few accolades when the death-or-glory boys are manning weapons up top. They keep the heart of the ship beating while the arms and legs are flailing about, and for the most part they are a reticent crowd; aloof from the antics of 'dabtoes'. Living in a twilight world of artificial light and the stench of oil, where steam and the heavy thrust of pistons dominate. When they do emerge into the daylight it is usually with a wad of cotton-waste in one hand and a spanner in the other, blinking at unaccustomed sunlight as they delve into remote corners of deck-machinery while seamen stand about impatiently, waiting for the taciturn aliens from the underworld to put things right for them.

There is time-honoured antipathy between the branches, going back to the time when steam took over from sail. A sort of tolerant rivalry that manifests in a lot of half-serious banter that seems to enhance rather than weaken the overall structure of a ship's company. Only when some nosy outsider threatens to interfere do the two sides join together in defence of their ship.

Right now Spiller works alongside us while his mates go off quietly to watch over the generator, knowing we are relying on them, and requiring no false, condescending plaudits from the deck-gang to spur them on to do their job.

One of the immigrants must have known how to 'break' the joining shackle and release the slip. So we have to veer out more cable until we can locate the next joining-link. This is no time for frugality so I just dump the spare cable overboard. This ship is doomed the moment she runs ashore, for no salvage company will find it worthwhile trying to save her. Everyone, including her owner/captain, accepts she is to be sacrificed for the lives of the immigrants, and one short length of anchor cable will be no loss to anyone.

We need two hands up here: one for the ship and one for

ourselves. More than once I feel my feet leave the deck as she drops into a deep valley, and I station a man especially to keep his eyes open for rogue waves so they do not overwhelm us before we can take a hold, and grip tightly to keep from being swept overboard. I no longer know or care how the immigrants fare in the waist. It must be hell down there, but now we all have our own battles to fight against the storm, and my only concern is to get the tow secured.

The wind tugs at us with a new venom, shrieking through the rigging with increased fury and building up advancing swells until they hang over us like cliffs. Every now and again a big one comes to blot out the sky and gloat over our puny craft before trying to crush the life out of her. At such times we clutch at the nearest handhold and stare up while she fights to ride the swell to see another thunderous cataract poised to smash down and crush the life out of her. Somehow she lifts and breaks clear with the sea draining from her scuppers while we use the brief respite to work furiously before the next one comes. At last I am able to cross my hands above my head to tell Border all is secure, and he orders the signalman to flash the message to the tug.

She makes a brave picture as she breasts the rollers and comes weltering down to us. At times her upperworks are invisible when she falls into a trough, then she lifts into sight with white foam spewing from every aperture. Her skipper knows what he is about and there is a purpose in the way he goes about picking up the tow. I can see her crew sheltering under the break of the fo'c'sle wearing lifebelts and waiting for the very last moment before venturing out. They've done it many times and know exactly what's required of them. I can see heaving lines being coiled and wonder why they are not using gun-lines in these conditions, then I get my answer when I see how her skipper uses his engines, watching in admiration the way he brings her stern close up on the windward side.

He holds her there while one of his seamen hurls a line over and drops it right across the fo'c'sle, sweet as you like.

Eager hands grab at it and soon the big eye of the hawser is snaking in through the fair-leads. As soon as the tug's skipper is certain we have it a swirl of white spreads from her squat stern and she surges forward. At one time she comes so close I can count the rivets on her side and it seems impossible that we will not collide. Already Henry has the hawser shackled to the cable and what follows is academic.

We ease out about thirty feet of cable and the tug draws ahead until there is a long bite between the two ships. The old freighter snubs at her bridle for a few minutes, reluctant to come to heel behind the small tug, but gradually she succumbs to the persistent pull and falls obediently into line-astern once more. Slowly, inevitably, we are being towed towards Israel, but no one pretends the party is over. I leave a couple of my lads with Henry to watch over the tow and take the remainder aft where Border is waiting on the port wing.

'Well done, Grant,' he says with feeling.

'I'd like to go down to help prepare the immigrants for disembarkation, sir. I don't think we can leave it to them. It is going to require co-operation because it looks as though we will have to ferry the weak and injured ashore in rafts and lifeboats when we get to the beach. Some of the worst will be on stretchers.'

For a moment I think he is going to refuse, and tell me it is up to the Jews to sort out their own mess, but he agrees in the end, and earns my respect for doing so.

'All right, Grant. I don't envy you going down there, but I think it is time we showed them our other side.'

He looks towards *Condor* as she circles slowly. 'I'd like to offer stretchers and medical supplies, but it would be suicide to attempt a transfer in these seas. Anyway, by what I've seen of these people I'm sure you will find them enterprising enough to provide make-shift stretchers and other means of getting everyone ashore. Try to explain that even when we get them to the beach their ordeal is not over.

The Monday Mutiny

The surf will be murderous, and it won't be an orderly evacuation by any stretch of the imagination.

'The strong must look after the weak and it must be organised so that everyone knows exactly where to fit in with the crowd. We will try to land in small groups, hoping that the shore authorities will be on hand to ensure no one drowns in the surf. You will have to work with the Jews, Grant. Try and find responsible people who can be relied upon to shepherd the immigrants ashore.'

'I would like to go too.' Morgan steps forward.

'Aren't you worried about your ship?' I sneer at him. 'After all, you did all this to pay off what you owed on her, didn't you?'

His face goes livid. 'I am still her master and owner I'll remind you. Those passengers down there are my responsibility and I intend to see them to their destination.'

I look at Border, expecting him to order Morgan back down into the cabin. I'm pretty certain he is on the point of doing so when he has a sudden change of heart. 'Go ahead, Grant. Captain Morgan is correct: this is his ship. Remember though, captain. You gave us your word.' Morgan nods curtly and goes below.

Before I can follow Border says quickly. 'About Monday, Coxswain. You know the book better than I do. Is "mutiny" too strong a charge?'

'He came up here with two armed men to help the immigrants take over the ship. He released the men we held in custody. He incited two of our own sailors to hand over their weapons – I can't think of any other word for it, sir. After all, I don't think you have to have a wholesale revolt to call it "mutiny".'

I leave him nodding pensively.

Eight

I find no lack of volunteers amongst *Condor*'s men, so I pick the nearest and go down with Morgan to where Caleb and a few of his mates are waiting for us by the hatch. For a moment I assume they are coming into the hold with us, but they just look on sullenly as we lower ourselves through the small opening. The picture established in my mind is made up of mental images created by the sounds and smells that reached us inside the wheelhouse. I am no stranger to claustrophobic conditions, and quite prepared for the tiers of wooden bunks that line the ship's side. It does not shock me to see tables and stools wrenched from their fastenings to float about in an ankle-deep morass of vomit and water, and smell the dank, humid stench of rancid humanity.

My imagination has not played down the grim reality, but I am not prepared for the suffering I see when my eyes adjust to the gloom. The pale faces peering out at me from the deep recesses hold no resentment for me and my lads: indeed, there is a kind of plaintive hope written in the features of many, while others register only despair.

Down here the truth hits me with a force that drives away the memory of terrorist bombs, and even dulls the anger that Robby's blindness left in me. God knows what some of them have lived through, or the indescribable brutality they have seen before they set eyes on this hell-ship. Now they look dejected and desperately sad, resigned to whatever destiny holds for them, retching on the dregs of their last meal with their bodies twisting in agony.

The Monday Mutiny

For a moment I am frozen in the midst of it all with my guts tied in a knot as the pathos takes form in remote corners. Whoever labelled these people 'illegal immigrants' should stand where I am and look into the sunken eyes. See these folk herded together like animals into the bowels of this excuse for a ship to face a murderous journey because no one wants to know about them. The sight would leave an indelible impression of tragedy and a deep sense of shame. I see no illegal immigrants here; only men, women and kids looking for somewhere to find peace and security. If that anonymous labeller feels like I do he will choke on his own words.

Shaking away these thoughts I look round for where to begin. It seems hopeless as I stand with the water slushing about my feet. We have about six hours to prepare them for their next ordeal. We don't know what facilities await us when we reach the coast. Border says all ports are closed to us between Haifa and Tel Aviv, but constant radio contact is being maintained with the authorities so that a reception committee should be there to meet us on the beach.

We must work on the assumption that we will have to use our rafts and boats to ferry the sick and weak to shore and lifelines for the strong to make their own way through the surf. We can expect no help from *Condor* or the other ships once we are in the shallows, and even if we manage to beach her properly it will be a bloody miracle if we get the sick and injured to safety without mishap.

'We must make stretchers and lash the injured to them,' I tell Morgan. 'Cover them with coats and blankets – anything we can find to keep them as dry as possible. The timber from the bunks will do to make the stretchers. Are there any handymen amongst this lot?'

'By what I've seen I'd say they can all turn their hands to whatever comes along. Snag is they speak about half a dozen languages, but once they have been given a lead there's no holding them.'

'Right then: if I get on with that perhaps you can

organise a bucket chain to bail out some of the water. I guess the pumps are working flat out, but they don't seem to cope with this.'

'They are inadequate. It was because they were so bloody useless during the storm the ballast shifted. I will work in the deep end and you can use the starboard side if you like.'

We are attracting some of the fitter immigrants now and they gather round while Morgan explains what we have in mind. In no time tools appear from odd corners and I find myself pushed further and further into the background as they start work. The hold resounds to the percussion of hammers and the rasp of saws. After a couple of experimental efforts they find the right formula and a production-line develops. Vacant bunks are cannibalised by the sawyers, and they begin to produce ready-made lengths of timber for the assemblers. Men, women, young and old, everyone fit enough joins in; even the kids fetch and carry, staggering across the heaving deck like veterans.

It is good to see, and their enthusiasm is contagious as I dodge about trying to help wherever I can. I sense the resilience of these people and know that one day there will be an Israel. But whether they will ever find peace is another matter.

The sound of industry attracts more Jews down from the upper-deck, until only Caleb and a dozen or so of his most ardent supporters remain aloof, resenting the fraternisation going on below.

Suddenly I find I am spending most of my time toddling about doing nothing of any value to anyone. In fact some of them make no effort to hide their impatience at my incompetence. I am no carpenter, and when it comes to preparing stretchers with belts and scarves to lash down the incapacitated even the women leave me standing. So, feeling totally rejected I signal Morgan that I am going up top to see what I can do up there. He gives an off-hand wave, but he is far too busy to bother with me, so I assume he has heard.

The full force of the storm slams into me when I stick my

head out of the hatch, and for a moment it takes my breath away, but I can see some of our lads working in the waist, securing loose lashings and stowing away gear while Caleb's men stand round disconsolately watching them. I go aft to find Border on the wheel with only the signalman beside him. A token line of armed seamen line the front of the bridge, but everyone seems to accept that the armistice is here to stay.

'I would like to release a couple of the lifeboats, sir,' I tell Border. 'We could use the davits to lower the stretchers over the side.'

He glances at the doubled-up boats. It is amazing that any have survived the storm. The only casualty is the lower one on the port davits which has been stove in.

'All right,' he says. 'That's a good idea. I had hoped to transfer them from the low side of the waist; it's almost at water-level, but if the sea is coming inboard it might be safer to use the davits. They will be that much closer to the beach anyway. I wondered about rigging a breeches-buoy, but that would take too long and some of the immigrants are too old or weak to use it. I'm afraid it is going to end up in a mad scramble despite all our efforts. We must try to keep some of the strongest back to help with the sick. The injured can be ferried ashore on carley-rafts. Hopefully the army will be waiting to give us a hand. Take as many men as you want down to the port davits and get rid of those boats.'

There is nothing fancy about these davits. They are just tapered metal tubes bent over at the top to form a curve, with no quick-release gear such as we have on our seaboats. God knows how anyone is supposed to lower the boats in an emergency, for the top one has to be cleared and lowered to the water before the falls can be hauled in again and hooked on to the lower boat. The Board of Trade would have a fit if they saw this lot.

'Get an axe!' I yell at a seaman. 'I'll cut through the falls and drop the whole bloody lot over the side.'

'What about this?' asks one of the others, brandishing a meat-cleaver.

'Where did that come from?'

He grins wickedly. 'I managed to salvage it, Swain. The bloke who was wavin' it abaht wasn't so lucky.'

I weigh it in my hand for a moment, studying the rigging. The falls look new as I would expect in this jury-rigged set-up, installed recently especially for this trip. The only projection on the smooth davits are metal cleats welded halfway up. I don't fancy using those as footholds, so it looks as though I will have to balance on the top guardrail and hang on to the smooth metal with one hand while I swing the cleaver with the other to hack away at the three-fold purchase. The guardrail doesn't inspire me with confidence either: it looks old, frayed and full of snags, sagging down in a deep loop, for no one has ever bothered to take up the slack on the 'tulips'.

I am no tightrope-walker, and when I place one foot tentatively on the wire it slumps down about ten inches and jerks wildly as I try to maintain balance. Eventually I end up with the ball of one foot placed precariously on the rounded top of one of the stanchions with one arm crooked round the davit, and a very nervous seaman holding on desperately to my legs. The wind immediately senses my plight and hurtles in sadistically to try to pluck me out into the ocean.

I take a deep breath and hold on tightly, waiting for a downward roll to ensure the boat will fall outboard when I slice through the falls. I miss a couple of chances while I dither about, trying to gain some sort of balance, and the ship heels over until my helpers are wading knee-deep making snide remarks about my lubberliness. On the next roll I brace up and go for it; swinging the cleaver like a tomahawk. The edge is razor-sharp but there are six lengths of rope to slice through. With any luck I might have chosen the right one and that would have done the trick, but that's too easy: the first one parts, whips back, and jams into the jaw of the pulley, so I have to hack through them all.

The boats hang there stubbornly, refusing to fall away while the ship rolls back to starboard. We hold our breath, praying they won't break loose now and crash in on the seamen. I sweat while I wait for her to recover and roll over to port again, but the bitch takes her time, as though she enjoys playing cat and mouse with us. Taking a grip on myself I wait while she makes up her mind and comes back to dig her port rails into the swell, then I lash out at the falls.

This time the falls part and if the gods were with me I would have succeeded in getting rid of at least one boat. Instead, the after end collapses as neat as you like into the wreckage of the lower boat. Too late I realise I should have had another man with an axe on the forward falls; it's easy to be wise after the event! Now I have to work forward past two tons of unpredictable wreckage to reach the other davit. The smashed timbers are splayed out like the petals of a gigantic, maneating flower, with jagged edges and lethal splinters. There is no chance of making a quick dash when the opportunity comes for I must wade through the mess while the sea swirls everything about my legs. All that keeps the boats from falling outboard now is the way they are trapped by the forward davit. Release that and everything should fall clear.

It is Dobwell who sees what needs to be done and heaves a rope at me. I grab at it, and when the next roll comes he and a mate haul me bodily across to them. While I struggle for breath and search about for a way to reach the forward falls Dobwell comes to my rescue again by suggesting, ' 'Ere, Swain. Let me put my foot in your 'ands.'

I have no will to argue with him. My body is bruised and battered by the wreckage and I have had enough of monkeying about with one foot in the air. Time is running out too for the wreckage could work loose at any second and break away in all directions. I hand him the cleaver and clasp my hands together to make a stirrup.

The Monday Mutiny

He hoists himself up until he has hold of the davit, waiting as I did for the right moment to strike. Other men are holding on to me so that I don't lose balance and take both of us over the side. Staring up through the spray I watch him measure the distance and tense with his cleaver raised. I see him hack at it once – twice – three times before it gives. He gives a startled cry as the davit suddenly swings outboard, twisting his arm away from its grip. For a moment he is frozen above me like a statue and I reach up to grab his legs as he sways in the wind; hoping he will come crashing in on top of me. He claws the air, screaming as the tangled boats slide outboard, taking him with them. I have a brief glimpse of flailing arms and legs in the boiling surf before they are wrenched out of reach. All that remains is a spreading mass of broken timber.

Shocked and numbed I allow the men to drag me into the wheelhouse where I crouch spluttering and trying to gulp air into my lungs. 'Bloody hell! Bloody, bloody hell!' I gasp as I struggle to recover.

'Take it easy, Coxswain,' says Border quietly, and I swing on him as he looks anxiously at me from the wheel.

'Take it easy nothing!' I scream at him. 'What the fucking hell is this all about anyway?' I fall back against the woodwork. Dobwell was indestructible – those old stripeys never die. He had been right through the war, and now he is dragged overboard from this rotten barge.

'What bowler-hatted moron dreamed this up?' I rave. 'What brilliant Admiralty genius sent us to sort out this bloody mess?' I am almost sobbing as my insides boil with fury and frustration, knowing that Dobwell was killed doing what I should have been doing. I am shaking: unable to clear my mind while visions of those whirling limbs torture my brain.

Border's tone is full of concern. 'It is nobody's fault, Grant. Recriminations will help no one. Get a hold of yourself. It is a straightforward task now, and we do not have to work out the rights and wrongs of it. All we have to do is get this ship to the beach and save as many lives as possible.'

I look as his anxious face as some of the fire drains away. 'Sorry, sir. It's just that Dobwell – well, it just seems so bloody useless.'

He smiles sadly. 'We all feel like that, Grant. The only thing to do is get on with the job. Perhaps by the time we have finished, our lords and masters will have worked out a solution.' He looks away when he reads the doubt in my face.

'I'd like to go down into the hold again, sir.'

He studies my face intently for a moment and I can see what is going through his mind even before he speaks. 'Do you think you are in the right frame of mind to go down there? You mustn't let Dobwell's death throw you. Don't take it out on innocent people, Coxswain.'

'It's nothing like that, sir. If we are going to work with these people I think it is time we got started.'

'All right,' he agrees. 'Away you go.'

Morgan and a few immigrants have things well in hand when I get below. One end of the hold is a welter of activity as the assembly-line continues to turn out stretchers. There is already a line of carefully cocooned immigrants spaced out on the deck close to the ladder leading up to one of the hatches, and the water-level on the port side is reduced so that tidal waves no longer surge across the area with every roll of the ship. Even the list doesn't seem so bad now that most of the immigrants are assembled on the starboard side, and we have lost the weight of the two port life-boats.

I gaze about me, wondering where best to start and suddenly find Monday standing beside me. He looks tired, red-eyed and unshaven: a reflection of myself no doubt.

'Captain Morgan thinks we should get some of the stretcher cases up top, Swain.' He talks calmly, as though things are perfectly normal and he has not committed one of the most serious crimes in the book.

'That is exactly why I came below. Those stretchers will

only just pass through the small opening so we won't want to be working while the ship is seething with bloody panic.' I look him straight in the eye. 'Border says you might do yourself a bit of good if you set to and work with us.' My voice is loaded with sarcasm. 'What about your star patient? Have you delegated your midwifery to someone else?'

'She's dead,' he says coldly. 'There's nothing more I can do there.'

He will get no sympathy from me. 'There's a hell of a lot to be done down here,' I snarl. 'And don't think this will get you off the hook. I hope for what you've done they make you rot in hell.'

I leave him and go over to Morgan. 'I'm told you want us to get some of these people up top?'

'That's right.' He straightens up, placing his fists into the small of his back and stretching out his cramped muscles. A porcelain face stares up at us from a stretcher: big sad eyes blinking from above the blankets, anxiously waiting to see what we are going to do next.

'Got any ideas about how to go about it?' he asks.

'When we off-load torpedoes from a submarine we rig runners. They make a sort of chute. I reckon that is the best way – we have loads of spare timber down here; it shouldn't be difficult. It will be a tight squeeze, but two planks side by side will do the trick, providing we have someone each side to guide them up. A couple of burly seamen on the upper deck can haul the stretchers up with rope.'

'Sounds fine to me,' he agrees heartily, adding an afterthought, 'Only stretcher cases though. The rest must remain below on this side or she will go top-heavy again.'

With that settled we get down to it, stowing the sick and injured along the starboard side where the after deckhouse provides a lee and a canvas cover protects them from the worst of the storm. Caleb and his cronies stay apart in a disgruntled group, but everyone ignores them while we get on with the job. It seems the Irgun is long on aggression and short on benevolence. Still, we are too busy to worry about their hang-ups.

The system works well. One by one the casualties emerge into the daylight, lying quiet for the most part, suffering our clumsy efforts without complaint when we knock them against hard metal corners as we stagger on the moving deck. When all is done I go and report to Border.

'There's the Palestine coast coming into detail now,' he says before I speak. 'It is going to be dicey turning her in the surf. Pity she is not built like our own landing-craft, we could have dropped the kedge over the stern and run the bow right up on the beach, but I dare not risk it with this ship. I will require both anchors to hold her bows up into the wind when the tug turns away. I'm hoping she will hang on to the tow and steady us as we go in. As soon as we can we must get stern-lines ashore before she broaches. If we end up beam on to this lot with the keel on the bottom we'll be in real trouble.'

He stares ahead as though he can visualise the situation. 'We will need to heave in the tow and put the hawser directly onto the bollards, Grant. That will give us a chance to re-shackle the cable before the tug goes about, so that we can use both anchors. With luck they will hold her head up-wind while we use the carley-rafts to float the stern-lines ashore. If the army is there they might have a jeep or two to tow the rafts through the surf. We are all going to get very wet; that's inevitable, but I assume there will be ambulances standing by, and medical staff available, so perhaps it won't be too bad.'

I make no reply as I look out at the coastline stretching featureless and drab across our bow. It looks like low, sandy-coloured clouds sitting on the horizon. If this is the Jews' promised land they can have it as far as I'm concerned. All I see is camel-country; fit only for vultures and nomads, and it's going to require more than a couple of watering-cans to make it attractive to my way of thinking.

The signal lamps are busy again as we near the shore,

spelling out orders for rounding up into the wind, and at last the big tug from Cyprus comes bustling over the western horizon, but we stick with her small sister while she hangs about in case she is needed. If the weather was halfway decent she could have hitched her bow to our stern and helped, but in these conditions that is out of the question.

The skipper of the small tug must have studied his chart well for he intends taking us to within three hundred yards of the beach before turning seaward, and promises to hold the tow as we drift aft with the wind. With both anchors holding we can ease out on the cables and control the drift. There is not enough tide in the Mediterranean to cause any worry, so it is a joint effort between the tug, our blokes on the fo'c'sle and providence.

Leading Seaman Henry is making a name for himself today. He is showing himself to be intelligent, with a full working knowledge of her anchors and cables. Soon he should be wearing the peaked cap of a PO if he carries on like this. An unpretentious man, it takes something unusual to bring him to the attention of his senior officers, and I wonder how many other Henrys are hiding beneath a façade of anonymity. I have confidence enough in him to leave him in charge while I carry out a roving commission; keeping myself available where I am most needed while Border stays aft with the bulk of the boarding party until we are safely beached.

With all that settled I start to grow more optimistic. True the coastline seems reluctant to come closer, but there is purpose to everything we do now, and with the list reduced to ten degrees things are a lot easier on deck. Only the wind stays malevolent as it drives in huge ranks of spume-laden coamers as though intent on wrecking our efforts even before we get to the shore. I hear a couple of infants wailing somewhere, but apart from them the immigrants are quietly going about their preparations now that they know their ordeal is coming to an end.

The Monday Mutiny

Morgan comes into the wheelhouse and stands looking out across the bow for a while in silence. There is no will on anyone's part to open up a conversation, so it is left to him to break the spell.

'They are a strange race when you think about it,' he muses, talking mostly to himself.

'How do you mean?' I prompt.

'Well, let's face it. Britain is made up of all kinds of different races: Normans, Saxons, Celts and God knows what else. They have all become absorbed into a new culture, producing a new race. There hasn't been an Israel since Roman times and some of these have lived in countries like Germany, Poland, Russia for generations – longer than the Normans or whatever; yet they still call themselves Jews.'

'That's right,' snorts the signalman. 'They're a pig-headed lot. Makes you wonder if they don't enjoy bein' persecuted. I sometimes think they bloody well thrive on it.'

Morgan laughs bitterly. 'Did you ever hear about Masada?' No one replies so he goes on.

'Masada was the last chunk of Israel left after Jerusalem was destroyed by the Romans. In this tiny piece of land one thousand Jews held out against an entire legion in the winter of 72/73 AD. The Romans had to build a big earth ramp to get at them, and when the Jews knew they had no chance they burned their gear and committed suicide. Every single one of them, group by group – one by one.'

'Bloody hell!' exclaims Bunts. 'What soddin' good did that do?'

'You would need to be a Jew to understand,' says Morgan with a grin. 'One thing you can be sure of though. No one is going to beat them. Hitler tried, Stalin tried, even the Caesars had a go, but they're still here.'

'Yeah, and still makin' a bloody nuisance of themselves,' growls another voice from the background. 'I live in Whitechapel and they're orl over the place. Why cain't they be like everyone else, fer God's sake?'

'They call it diaspora,' explains Morgan. 'They spread out all over the world but always remain Jews. That's why few of them marry Gentiles.'

The same nasal, protesting voice goes on from the back, 'Every damn business rahned our way is run by the bloody Jews, an' nah they wants ter take over Palestine.'

'It's their promised land.'

'Tell that ter the Arabs!' growls Bunts, bringing the talk round full circle, and everyone goes quiet again, allowing the wind to call the tune with its mournful whining.

Cheetah's lamp blinks more instructions for the final leg of the operation. She and *Condor* will try to make a lee for us when the time comes to turn the ship, and the big tug offers to pump oil in an attempt to smooth out the surf during the critical moments when we will be broadside to wind and sea. Border rejects this offer because of the danger to immigrants who might have to swim through the stuff if it drifts down to them.

The first and most crucial part will come when the little tug tries to bring our bow upwind. I look astern at the lifting hillocks of boiling ocean bearing down to devour us. There must be more that we can do to prepare for beaching. Those waves will be thundering on the shore with the conflicting forces of the undertow building them up into walls of white-crested breakers, big enough to overpower the little ship when she lies powerless in the shallows. My mind paints a frightening picture of her stuck hard on her beam-ends with a huge crest looming over her like a cliff.

'I think we should make ready now,' Borders says quietly, echoing my own thoughts. We can see serried ranks of surf ahead as the shore seems suddenly much closer, with outcrops of rock reaching out to starboard. It is a scene of devastation as the ship rides up on a confluence of conflicting swells, lifting to give a panoramic view of the wide-sweeping bay.

I go forward to Henry and his cable-party. Caleb and his mates watch sour-faced as I go by, and I get a sudden momentary chill in my back. They must know what is happening to the Irgun terrorists who fall into the army's clutches and will expect no mercy. I make a mental note to keep an eye on them when we land.

The ship groans and shudders, bringing my thoughts back to the present. We are buffeted by shorter seas now as we feel the counteraction of the shallows. The movement is less predictable as she struggles in conflicting forces with broken water all about her. Five toots on the tug's siren warn that she is about to make her turn. The towing hawser jerks taut, sings loud for a moment, then goes slack again as the bow begins to swing. Her men are taking in the slack on their big towing winch to shorten the tow. Henry's men are doing the same so they can 'break' the cable and re-connect it to the anchor. The shorter span gives the tug more immediate control over us, but it also increases the risk of parting, and I notice Henry urging his lads to make preparations for letting go the anchors in a hurry if that should happen. He doesn't miss a trick.

The little tug makes a plucky picture as she bores into the sea, making a wide circle and plunging into the swells, so that at times she is completely hidden from us by explosions of bursting spray. She shakes clear with her stern awash with foam, and we see her crew crouching under the over-hang. We have to squint through blinding spray as it lashes into our raw faces, while our legs bend and stretch to counteract the mad antics of the ship. Once more the tow-line snaps bar-taut, wringing fountains of spray from its strands as it sings with the strain. Everyone holds his breath; a straining hawser can become a vicious reptile if it cuts loose. I feel the judder as the ship fights against the pull, trying to fall away from a succession of breakers.

Now the full force of the storm smashes into our port side, hurling white water waist-deep across the hatches to search into every corner with its hungry talons, clutching all in its path. Caleb and his men flatten their bodies to the deck and cling on desperately. God knows how the poor devils on the stretchers are faring – the only comfort is that they are placed in the least vulnerable part of the well-deck, but even so they must find themselves submerged for long periods. There's little time to dwell on that before another monster sweeps in to engulf the ship and thunder along the whole length, burying her in a welter of swirling ocean.

Surely she cannot survive much more of this! I feel the sucking pull of the wave as it grabs at my legs, threatening to tear me away from my hold. I hear screaming, highpitched and panic-stricken, from the waist, along with the crashing of loose gear. For an eternity the ship is at the mercy of that huge sea, keeled over until the deck seems almost vertical, with the roar of the storm filling our ears while we grope and gasp for life. There is nothing to do but hold on grimly, for the little ship is completely overwhelmed as tons of water thump down on her, intent on holding her down in readiness for the next mountain to sweep in to finish her off.

Mercifully it doesn't come, and we are spared by a quirk of nature as two conflicting forces merge and sap each other's power before they hit us, coming together right beneath our keel so we are lifted vertically and held in their grip for long seconds, twisting and turning on the apex of the two swells until the tug drags our bow upwind and we slide head-first into the trough.

After that the onslaught meets us squarely on the bow, pushing our stern away so that we face into the storm, held steady by that single wire and the sturdy little tug.

As if in triumph the tug toots at us with a long, impelling wail that comes down on the wind to trigger Leading Seaman Henry into action.

No need for me or any other senior officer to tell him what needs to be done. Almost before the sound fades he swings his maul on to the pelican hook so that it snaps open to release the cable, sending the port anchor rattling out of the hawsepipe with a cloud of rust. Its comforting roar rising above the storm.

The Monday Mutiny

I stay well back and let the experts go about their business. The wind shrieks its outrage as we wait for a moment before letting go the starboard anchor. Already we are falling astern, although it is impossible to tell if the anchors are holding. Border leaves it entirely to Henry's judgement and he eases out the cable at precisely the right speed.

She is like a tigress when she realises what is happening and tries to wrench free of her bridle. She flings herself from side to side as she strives to break the flukes out of the sea-bed. I can feel her snubbing viciously at the cables as she throws her tantrum, but we have the bitch in hand now, and the storm can only help us as it drives her stern towards the beach. The seas break continuously over the whole ship, but link by link we are drifting aft and I can already make out the features of the shore as we hit the surf. We have come right in to the mouth of a wide, sweeping bay.

I hear hooters, and when I look towards the beach I feel like cheering as I see a long line of vehicles, with headlights blazing, drawn up along the coast road. Thank God the army's there. I feel the first jar as her keel hits the sand, lifts, then surges astern on the crest of a big sea before thumping down to hold fast on the beach. We are much too far out for the heaving-lines, so I leave Henry to it and clamber down from the fo'c'sle yelling at the men to help clear away the carley-rafts.

The moment it splashes into the surf I am prepared to leap aboard with a line, then suddenly Monday bundles past with a rope wrapped round his waist, shouting into my ear as he pushes by, 'Let me go, Swain. I can swim through that lot quicker than the raft will drift in. It's what I'm best at – swimming.'

No time to argue for he is already halfway over the gun'l. I grab at the line and prepare to feed it through my hands.

'I'll do better without this,' he shouts, stripping off his rubber lifebelt and plunging into the surf. He wasn't kidding when he said he could swim; he goes through the surf with long, powerful strokes, clawing at the bottom with his feet when the sea sets him down. He uses the breakers to lift him towards the men on the sand, and they wade out chest deep to meet him as he reaches the shallows. The line is snaking through my hands as they haul it in and attach it to a winch on one of the four-wheel-drive 'quads'. Now I can send the main tackle in on the carley-raft, and soon we have a hawser running through a pulley on the davit to a snatch-block on shore so that the army can haul the raft in and out from the beach, leaving our own men to help the immigrants as they go.

More lifelines are snaking out to shore, and more carley-rafts splash down to back the one we are using. I see the army manoeuvering a Land-Rover to haul them in when they are loaded.

The waves are roaring in and lifting the ship so that we need to watch every movement we make, but each time she is set down further up onto the beach and the slack is quickly taken in on the stern-lines so that she is made more secure with every surge. Eventually movement ceases altogether, and she lies hard on the sand with the waves bursting over her. It is time to get the weak and wounded ashore now, starting with the ones from the hold who are able to walk, and we form a double line of the fittest to feed them through to the rafts. It is made more simple because the port waist is almost at water-level and we can send them ashore half a dozen at a time, with sailors wading shoulder deep to steady them on the raft as they are ferried through the breakers. The immigrants have organised themselves so that the more able ones alternate with the old and infirm on the lifelines, and they are using the spare rafts on the starboard side for mothers with small children. I am so busy I have not noticed the sun go down. We are working in the glow of headlamps from a crescent of vehicles spaced out on the beach.

We are well under way when Monday comes to yell in

my ear again. 'I think I would be more use with those still waiting on the stretchers, Swain.'

'Do what you bloody well like,' I snarl. 'I'm not interested in what you have to do or say.' I stare belligerently at him for a moment with spray running down my face. His face is gaunt in the shadowy light, and I see he is exhausted like the rest of us, but I have no compassion. I see only a louse who let his mates down when he was most needed, and cannot be depended upon to do his duty. There is no room in my navy for individuals like him, and nothing he can do now will change my mind. We are all sickened and tired by what we have seen and done and his 'holier than thou' attitude just makes it worse. I push my face close to his to grate, 'You had best keep out of my sight, Monday. I hope they throw the book at you when this is all over, you mutinous bastard!'

The incident has brought back all the rage that came when Dobwell went overboard. The work had driven it beneath the surface for a time; now it is there again, boiling up so that the huddled shapes of the immigrants no longer arouse any sympathy in me. I find myself urging them along impatiently, manhandling the slower ones to keep them moving, and squeezing more and more into each raft, anxious to be rid of them, until a shout of alarm comes from one of my own men when he sees the danger.

For a second or so I stare outraged at the presumptive young OD who has the temerity to shout at his coxswain, and I am about to give him a roasting when my eye is caught by a wretched face staring up from beneath a black hood. There is no malice or resentment in the expression. The old lady just looks sadly at me, as though I have destroyed her illusion that all military are not like the evil bastards with the death's head badges on their caps. A hot flush of shame reddens my face as I look at her, knowing that for one moment I was consumed with a blind hate for her and her kind. In those few minutes they were a bloody nuisance to me, and I realise this is part of the problem for them: when they are not being kicked about, or shoved into gas chambers, they are just a bloody nuisance.

I place my hand on her arm gently, holding her steady while the raft bobs about alongside. I feel her weak, skeletal, fragile limbs responding to my touch, and the men in the water reach up to guide her rickety frame into place. She sits there looking up at me: stricken and soaked through as she settles on the bottom-boards with water slushing over her. She accepts what is happening to her with a blind faith and the last thing she needs is some ill-tempered sod like me badgering her along. I have never felt so lousy in my life.

After that I work like an automaton. Moving people along as though on a conveyor-belt; oblivious to the stinging bite of the spray or the buffeting wind. I feel sick and weary. There is nothing in this for me now. I'm saving lives but it makes no odds. All I want is to get back to sailoring again for I have no stomach left for this.

The sudden, strident rattle of gunfire knifes into my brain and jerks me out of my thoughts. People are screaming and falling over themselves to find cover. I dive with them to the deck and crouch peering over huddled shapes that are strewn like bundles of rags all over the place. The firing comes again and I spot the flashes somewhere close to the wheelhouse above me. The blinding glare of a searchlight sweeps in from the shore and dodges about the superstructure. Below me in the gap between the hatch-coaming and the front of the bridge there are still quite a number of stretcher cases lying in their cocoons. Border and the signalman are flattened against the steel bulkhead while Caleb and his men aim stens at their bellies. There is blood on the navigator's face and his uniform is torn.

Someone wriggles up to lie alongside me and when I look I see it is Henry. 'How the hell did that happen?' I ask.

'Easy enough, I reckon, Swain. We were much too busy to notice the lousy bastards taking advantage of the chaos.'

The Monday Mutiny

I recall the look I saw on Caleb's face and the thrill of anxiety that ran through me. I should have known then that he and his mob would never tamely surrender to the army. It is my bloody fault because I was too busy losing my temper to see what was going on. It must have been easy for them to disarm the few blokes left up on the bridge. It wouldn't have been difficult to conceal some of the weapons when the collection was made by our lads. We have been sloppy, and now we deserve all we get.

The situation is static as we wait for Caleb to make the next move. It looks like Border is quite seriously hurt for he slumps almost unconscious against the signalman, oozing blood from a headwound. The other members of his bridge-party are disarmed and stand shame-faced to one side, watched over by one of Caleb's men. We have been caught with our pants down, mainly due to my own stupid negligence.

When the hubbub subsides Caleb steps forward with his faithful translator. He holds the lad squarely in front of him as he dictates his message. He is a cold-blooded swine and wants to be sure we fully understand his terms. I pray that some trigger-happy so-and-so doesn't start a wholesale slaughter, for some of our men are holding weapons they have taken from the deck-locker.

'We do not wish to go with the army,' pipes the youngster's voice, loud enough for all to hear. 'We want one of the trucks and we will take your officer and two others for hostages and release them after one hour if we are not followed.'

Caleb issues further instructions and the lad goes on, 'If you do not grant this, some of the stretcher cases will die and their blood will be on your hands.' He waits for one more curt message from his boss. 'If you do not carry out these orders your officer will be the first to die.'

Everyone switches their attention to me. The army officers are out of earshot on the beach and Border is almost in a coma, so the weight is on my shoulders.

'I will pass your message to the army, Caleb. They are in control now.'

The huddled shapes are cautiously lifting from the deck to see what goes on as he absorbs my words and we wait while the wind batters the ship, sending clouds of spray sweeping across her decks. He mutters something through the corner of his mouth.

'That will not do,' quotes the lad stridently. 'We do not wish to talk with any more Englishmen.'

I am conscious of pale faces staring up at me. Most of the immigrants cannot understand what we are talking about, but they all know their lives are at stake. There is only one man I can fully trust to pass on the terms, and explain what is happening to the puzzled officers on the beach. I turn towards Henry.

'Caleb!'

The shout drags all eyes to the bridge where Monday stands in the blinding shaft of a searchlight, holding a naked new-born baby aloft in his hands while he stares down at the Jews, looking like a crazy-man with his hair streaming in the wind and the small doll-like shape wailing above his head.

'Are you going to murder this one too, Caleb?' he shouts. 'This is part of your new Israel. The birth of a nation!' He thrusts the minute, squawking infant forward so that we can all see its tiny legs kicking as it squirms in his hands.

We are all stunned into shocked silence as he lowers the baby to his chest and covers it with a cloth before tucking it into the crook of his arm and climbing slowly down the ladder. Caleb rattles the bolt of his sten threateningly, but his men stand spell-bound as Monday walks towards them. His eyes never leave the Jew's face, and even when the weapon is raised menacingly he doesn't hesitate. They face each other transfixed, two yards apart.

For a moment even the storm seems to hold its breath, then without another word Monday throws the baby at Caleb and the weapon clatters to the deck as the rebel's reflexes take over and he gathers the small shape in his arms.

Immediately the tension drops as the Irgun men are overpowered by their own kind before they come out of their trance, to be dragged none too gently into a safe corner. The disembarkation goes like clockwork after that, with the immigrants as anxious as we are to get the work done before any further gunplay takes place.

The army has everything in hand on the beach and there are Jewish representatives amongst them to get the immigrants into the waiting lorries. I watch Morgan being led away between two grim-faced red-caps. He stands to lose everything and spend up to eight years in prison for his part in the affair, but he manages a grin when he sees me staring at him.

Stretcher cases are being loaded into ambulances, while others climb over tailboards and sit staring out into the gloom at the first sight of their promised land. It is a cold-blooded process as the army goes about its task with quiet efficiency. Caleb and his mates get their wish, for they are given a truck to themselves; the only snag is the two armed sentries that watch over them, and the handcuffs on their wrists.

I fuss over the medical orderlies who are carefully placing Subby and Border into an ambulance. Subby seems reasonably comfortable but Border is unconscious and his face is the colour of parchment. In answer to my query one of the orderlies shakes his head sadly. 'We will be lucky to reach hospital with him, Chief. I'm sorry.'

We have been allocated two three-tonners at the rear of the convoy, but before we move off I run down the line of trucks looking for one man who I find arguing the toss with a corporal.

'Monday!' I snarl at him, and both men turn to face me. 'You are under open arrest. Come with me.'

Ignoring the raised eyebrows of the corporal Monday sighs and comes with me as meek as a lamb. The soldier watches him saunter across and calls over to me, 'That's right, Jack. Take the silly sod wiv yer. He arsks too many bloody questions.'

'I only wanted to know where they are taking the Jews,' protests Monday.

'Ter Athlit Internment camp o' course – where'd yer think, fer Christ's sake!' blares the corporal.

'Come on,' I growl, and he follows obediently towards our truck, to take his place on the bench seat and stare out impassively at a group of Arabs who seem to have materialized out of the desert to stand in the gloom. There is light enough to show the hatta and agal each one wears on his head, and the long gallabria of true Palestinians. As the convoy moves off we see more of them staring out of the velvet night where the desert rolls away to the east.

Monday turns to me. 'Do you think they will ever live together in peace?' he asks pensively.

'Not if I was an Arab they wouldn't,' I snarl harshly, then add in softer tone. 'You're not the only one who feels for the Jews, Monday, but no one's entitled to walk into another man's country and just take over. Christ, we've just fought a war to stop that happening to us!'

'I'm up to my neck now, aren't I?'

'Damn right you are!'

'Well I'm glad they reached Palestine, and we didn't tow them to Cyprus.'

We lapse into silence, half dozing as the truck rumbles along the coast road. Eventually it drops below the height of the ridge, hiding the sea as we move in through the suburbs of Haifa. We grind our way through narrow streets and I begin to come out of my stupor when I realise we are heading towards the harbour. We jolt through the dockyard and judder to a stop on the quay where the high flank of a merchant ship dominates.

'You can get down and stretch your legs if you like.' A soldier unlatches the tailboard and drops it down for us.

As I stretch my cramped muscles and stare about me an

The Monday Mutiny

angry babble of sound comes from the row of trucks. 'What's that all about?' I ask the soldier.

He glances over his shoulder at me. 'They've just found out where they are being taken.'

'Where's that?' asks Monday.

The soldier grins. 'They are being shipped out.'

'To Cyprus?'

'Cyprus be damned! That's the *Empire Rival*: she's taking them back to where they came from – Europe.'

The noise is growing as the news spreads from truck to truck. The army is already transferring the immigrants to the ship. Most go quietly; shuffling along resignedly, but others protest every step of the way. I watch two squaddies hoist a man up by his armpits when he throws himself to the ground and refuses to move. They haul him face down with his toes dragging in the dirt and bundle him over the gangway. It is a sickening spectacle, and all I can do is watch helplessly as they are herded like cattle into the ship.

'Watch out – he's got a revolver!'

The shout cuts into the dry air and my reflexes take charge as I dive for cover behind the double wheels of the truck. Monday slams into my side and we crouch together, sweating and peering out into the empty space where one lone, pathetic figure staggers splay-legged and uncertain, with a huge service revolver looking monstrous in his small hands. It is Caleb's translator, wide-eyed and terrified. Alone in the centre of the arena where hundreds of eyes stare out at him. I hear the metallic click of bolts as the soldiers take aim at him.

'Caleb!' he cries, the words half choked as he stares wildly about him.

'Jesus Christ!' I feel Monday tense up beside me. 'They'll shoot the poor little bastard!'

'Leave it!' I growl harshly. 'It's nothing to do with you.'

'Caleb – Caleb!' The animated figure is twirling about, his face twisted into a tortured mask as tears streak the dirt on his cheeks.

'Drop the revolver!' yells a heavy voice from somewhere. 'Drop it or we'll fire!'

There is no reason left in the lad's mind. He yells his anguish into the empty atmosphere and fires into space. A burst of automatic fire rattles out and the small figure is turned into a dancing puppet as the bullets thud into him. I feel Monday wrench away, and before I can stop him he is out there, racing towards the twirling shape. I see the wounds blossom like poppies on his white shirt as the lad's dead fingers squeeze the trigger.

Without thinking I leap up and run like a madman towards the two crumpled bodies lying in the dust. Their mixed blood is oozing into the dirt as I kneel down beside them. The lad is dead. His chest and throat torn out by the bullets. Monday lies across him, and I hear him groan as I bend down close to look.

Other figures are crowding round now; their shadows fall across our little group. Gently I roll Monday clear and place my rolled-up jacket under his head. His eyes stare up at me, filled with pain and despair. 'Oh, Mother of God!' he breathes. 'I've had it this time, Swain.'

'Don't be daft,' I lie. 'You're going to be okay.'

His mouth twists into a wry grin, then dribbles blood as he chokes. He winces as a sharp pain grips his body, and I wait, holding on to his shoulders while the convulsions subside, then he looks at me again.

'Don't let the army have me, Swain.'

'I won't mate. I'll stay with you.'

That seems to relax him and he lies back for a moment. I can sense the pain leaving him now. Suddenly there is a new light in his eyes, and he says in a stronger, angry voice, 'Just one thing, Grant.'

'What's that?'

But the effort is too much. His eyes widen for a second while his face relaxes. I have to bend closer, so that my ear is almost on his mouth. There is hardly a whisper of breath, but his eyes still flicker with life as he strives desperately to speak.

'What is it, Monday?' I urge quietly.

He makes one more vain effort to force out the words, but they refuse to come, and his body slumps back as he breathes one last, rattling sigh. I straighten up to find Jimmy standing by my side, immaculate in whites, as though he has just stepped ashore from the cutter.

'What did he say?' he asks.

'He said, "Sod the lot of them!" ' I snarl, and walk away.